Real-Life English

A COMPETENCY–BASED ESL PROGRAM FOR ADULTS

Program Consultants

Jayme Adelson-Goldstein
North Hollywood Learning Center
North Hollywood, California

Patricia De Hesus-Lopez
Texas A & M University
Kingsville, Texas

Julia Collins
Los Angeles Unified School District
El Monte-Rosemead Adult School
El Monte, California

Federico Salas-Isnardi
Houston Community College
Adult Literacy Programs
Houston, Texas

Else V. Hamayan
Illinois Resource Center
Des Plaines, Illinois

Connie Villaruel
El Monte-Rosemead Adult School
El Monte, California

Kent Heitman
Carver Community Middle School
Delray Beach, Florida

Wei-hua (Wendy) Wen
Adult & Continuing Education
New York City Board of Education
New York, New York

STECK-VAUGHN
C O M P A N Y
A Subsidiary of National Education Corporation

◆ ACKNOWLEDGMENTS

Staff Credits:

Executive Editor	◆	Ellen Lehrburger
Senior Editor	◆	Tim Collins
Design Manager	◆	Richard Balsam
Cover Design	◆	Richard Balsam
Photo Editor	◆	Margie Foster

Photo Credits:

Cover: James Minor, Cooke Photographics (title); © Randal Alhadeff–p.74, 86, 87d, 88, 114-116, 128, 129d; Bob Daemmrich–p.58, 59a, 59c, 73a; © Jack Demuth–p.4, 87a, 89a, 89b, 132; © Stephanie Huebinger–p.129b; © Zigy Kaluzny–p.92, 98b, 100, 102, 130; © John Langford–p.16-18, 22, 31d, 32, 53, 54, 73c; Phyllis Liedecker–p.3b, 3c, 3d, 27, 101, 129a, 136; Joan Menschenfreund–p.44; James Minor–p.2, 3a; © Park Street–p.59a and b, 73b, 104; © Daniel Thompson Photography–p.6, 39, 40, 41, 46, 55, 60, 63, 64.

Additional Photography by:

P.30, 31c, 42 Library of Congress; p.31a Northwind Picture Archives; p.35, 43, 56c, 56d The National Archives; p.45b © Richard Balsam; p.45d © Robert Brenner/PhotoEdit; p.50 © Robert Brenner/PhotoEdit; p.56a © Dennis McDonald/PhotoEdit; p.56b © Batt Johnson/Unicorn; p.59d © Michael Newman/PhotoEdit; p.72, 73d © Frances M. Cox/Stock Boston; p.87b and 87c Puget Sound, Power & Light Company; p.89c, 89d, 98a, 98c, 129c © Richard Balsam.

Illustration Credits:

The Ivy League of Artists, Inc.

Electronic Production:

International Electronic Publishing Center, Inc.

Contributing Writer to the First Edition:

Lynne Lilley Robinson
Division of Adult and Continuing Education
Sweetwater Union High School District, Chula Vista, California

CONTENTS

Real-Life English is a complete competency-based, four-skill program for teaching ESL to adults and young adults. *Real-Life English* follows a competency-based syllabus that is compatible with the CASAS and MELT (BEST Test) competencies, as well as state curriculums for competency-based adult ESL from Texas and California.

Real-Life English is designed for students enrolled in public or private schools, in learning centers, or in institutes, and for individuals working with tutors. The program consists of four levels plus a Literacy Level for use prior to or together with Level 1. *Real-Life English* has these components:

♦ Five Student Books (Literacy and Levels 1–4).

♦ Five Teacher's Editions (Literacy and Levels 1–4), which provide detailed suggestions on how to present each section of the Student Book in class.

♦ Four Workbooks (Levels 1–4), which provide reinforcement for each section of the Student Books.

♦ Audiocassettes (Literacy and Levels 1–4), which contain all dialogs and listening activities in the Student Books. This symbol on the Student Book page indicates each time material for that page is on the Audiocassettes. A transcript of all material recorded on the tapes but not appearing directly on the Student Book pages is at the back of each Student Book and Teacher's Edition.

Each level consists of ten units. Because the unit topics carry over from level to level, *Real-Life English* is ideal for multi-level classes.

 The *About You* symbol, a unique feature, appears on the Student Book page each time students use a competency. To facilitate personalization, color is used in dialogs and exercises. After students have learned a dialog or completed an exercise, they can easily adapt it to talk or write about themselves by changing the words in color.

Organization of Student Book 4

Each unit contains these eleven sections:

Unit Opener

Each Unit Opener includes a list of unit competencies, a photo and accompanying questions, and a dialog, a brief story, or a short article. (In Level 1 only, a chant always appears on this page.) Teachers can use the list of competencies for their own reference, or they can have students read it so that they, too, are aware of the unit's goals. The photo and questions activate students' prior knowledge by getting them to think and talk about the unit topic. The dialog, article, or story gets students reading, thinking, and talking about the unit topic.

Starting Out

Starting Out presents most of the new competencies, concepts, and language in the unit. It generally consists of captioned pictures, questions, and an *About You* activity.

Talk It Over

Talk It Over introduces additional competencies, language, and concepts, usually in the form of a dialog. The dialog becomes the model for an interactive *About You* activity.

Word Bank

Word Bank presents and develops vocabulary. The first part of the page contains a list of the new key words and phrases grouped by category. The Useful Language box contains common expressions, clarification strategies, and idioms students use in the unit. Oral and written exercises and *About You* activities provide purposeful and communicative reinforcement of the new vocabulary.

Listening

The Listening page develops competency-based listening comprehension skills. Tasks include listening to invitations, household safety instructions, doctors' advice, and car maintenance advice.

All the activities develop the skill of **focused listening.** Students learn to recognize the information they need and to listen selectively for only that information. They do not have to understand every word; rather, they have to filter out everything except the information they want to find out. This essential skill is used by native speakers of all languages.

Many of the activities involve **multi-task listening.** Students listen to the same selection several times and complete a different task each time. First they might listen for the main idea. They might listen again for specific information. They might listen a third time in order to draw conclusions or make inferences.

Culminating discussion questions allow students to relate the information they have heard to their own needs and interests.

Reading

The selections in Reading, such as advice columns, magazine and newspaper articles, apartment safety checklists, and employee benefit handbooks, focus on life-skill based tasks. Exercises, discussion questions, and *About You* activities develop reading skills and help students relate the content of the selections to their lives.

Structure Base

Structure Base, a two-page spread, presents key grammatical structures that complement the unit competencies. Language boxes show the new language in a clear, simple format that allows students to make generalizations about the new language. Oral and written exercises provide contextualized reinforcement of each new grammar point.

Writing

On the Writing page students develop authentic writing skills, such as writing invitations and thank-you notes, making entries in a checkbook register, completing a voter registration card, and writing a classified ad.

One To One

Each One To One section presents a competency-based information-gap activity. Students are presented with incomplete or partial information that they must complete by finding out the missing information from their partners. Topics include talking about bank services, discussing community issues, and asking about workplace rules. In many units, culminating discussion questions encourage students to relate the information they gathered to their own needs and interests.

Extension

The Extension page enriches the previous instruction with activities at a slightly more advanced level. As in other sections, realia is used extensively. Oral and written exercises and *About You* activities help students master the competencies, language, and concepts, and relate them to their lives.

Check Your Competency

The Check Your Competency pages are designed to allow teachers to track students' progress and to meet schools' or programs' learner verification needs. All competencies are tested in the same manner they are presented in the units, so formats are familiar and non-threatening, and success is built in. The list of competencies at the top of the page alerts teachers and students to the competencies that are being evaluated. The check-off boxes allow students to track their success and gain a sense of accomplishment and satisfaction.

 This *Check Up* symbol on the Check Your Competency pages denotes when a competency is evaluated. For more information on this section, see "Evaluation" on page viii.

Placement

Any number of tests can be used to place students in the appropriate level of *Real-Life English*. The following tables indicate placement based on the CASAS and MELT (BEST Test) standards.

Student Performance Levels	CASAS Achievement Score	Real-Life English
	164 or under	Literacy
I	165–185	Level 1
II	186–190	
III	191–196	Level 2
IV	197–205	
V	206–210	Level 3
VI	211–216	
VII	217–225	Level 4
VIII	226 (+)	

Teaching Techniques

Presenting Dialogs

To present a dialog, follow these suggested steps:

♦ Play the tape or say the dialog aloud two or more times. Ask one or two simple questions to make sure students understand.

♦ Say the dialog aloud line-by-line for students to repeat chorally, by rows, and then individually.

♦ Have students say or read the dialog together in pairs.

♦ Have several pairs say or read the dialog aloud for the class.

Presenting Articles

To present the brief articles in the Unit Openers, follow these steps:

♦ Have students use the photograph and the unit title to make predictions about what the article might be about. Restate the students' ideas and/or write them on the board in acceptable English.

♦ Play the tape or read the article aloud as students follow along in their books.

♦ Ask a few simple questions to make sure that students understood the main ideas. Have students refer to the predictions written on the board. Ask them to say which of the predictions were correct.

♦ Have them read the article again independently.

♦ Discuss the article with students. Ask additional comprehension questions. You might also ask the class to summarize the article, to state their opinions about it, or to state whether they agree with everything in the article.

Presenting Stories

To present the stories in the Unit Openers, follow these steps.

♦ Have students use the photograph and the unit title to make inferences about what the story might be about. Have them scan the story for the names of the characters. Have students talk about what the relationship among the people might be and what the story might say about them. Write their ideas on the board or restate them in acceptable English.

♦ Play the tape or read the story aloud as students follow along in their books.

♦ Ask a few simple questions to make sure that students understood the main ideas. Have students refer to the inferences you have written on the board. Ask them to say which of the inferences were correct.

♦ Have them read the story again independently.

♦ Discuss the story with students. Ask additional comprehension questions. You might also ask students to summarize the story or to say if they or anyone they know has had experiences similar to the ones in the story.

Reinforcing Vocabulary

To reinforce the words in the list on the Word Bank page, have students look over the list. Clarify any words they do not recognize. To provide additional reinforcement, use any of these techniques:

♦ **Vocabulary notebooks.** Have students use each new word to say a sentence for you to write on the board. Have students copy all of the sentences into their vocabulary notebooks.

♦ **Personal dictionaries.** Students can start personal dictionaries. For each new word students can write a simple definition and/or draw or glue in a picture of the object or the action.

♦ **Flash cards.** Flash cards are easy for you or for students to make. Write a new word or phrase on the front of each card. Provide a simple definition or a picture of the object or action on the back of the card. Students can use the cards to review vocabulary or to play a variety of games, such as Concentration.

♦ **The Remember-It Game.** Use this simple memory game to review vocabulary of every topic. For example, to reinforce food words, start the game by saying, *We're having a picnic, and we're going to bring apples.* The next student has to repeat the list and add an item. If someone cannot remember the whole list or cannot add a word, he or she has to drop out. The student who can remember the longest list wins.

Presenting Listening Activities

Use any of these suggestions:

♦ To activate students' prior knowledge, have them look at the illustrations, if any, and say as much as they can about them. Encourage them to make inferences about the content of the listening selection.

♦ Have students read the directions. To encourage them to focus their listening, have them read the questions so that they know exactly what to listen for.

♦ Play the tape or read the Listening Transcript aloud as students complete the activity. Rewind the tape and play it again as necessary.

♦ Check students' work.

In multi-task listenings, remind students that they will listen to the same passage several times and answer different questions each time. After students complete a section, check their work (or have students check their own or each others' work) before you rewind the tape and proceed to the next section.

Prereading

To help students read the selections with ease and success, establish a purpose for reading and call on students' prior knowledge to make inferences about the reading. Use any of these techniques:

♦ Have students look over and describe any photographs, realia, and/or illustrations. Ask them to use the illustrations to say what they think the selection might be about.

♦ Have students read the title and any heads or sub-heads. Ask them what kind of information they think is in the selection and how it might be organized. Ask them where they might encounter such information outside of class and why they would want to read it.

♦ Have students read the questions that follow the selection to help them focus their reading. Ask them what kind of information they think they will find out when they read. Restate their ideas and/or write them on the board in acceptable English.

♦ Remind students that they do not have to know all the words in order to understand the selection. Then have students complete the activities on the page. Check their answers.

One To One

To use these information gap activities to maximum advantage, follow these steps:

♦ Put students in pairs, assign the roles of A and B, and have students turn to the appropriate pages. Make sure that students look only at their assigned pages.

♦ Present the dialog in Step 1. Follow the instructions in "Presenting Dialogs" on page vi. (Please note that as these conversations are intended to be models for free conversation, they are not recorded on the Audiocassettes.)

♦ When students can say the dialog with confidence, model Step 2 with a student. Remind students that they need to change the words in color to adapt the dialog in 1 to each new situation. Then have students complete the activity.

♦ Have students continue with the remaining steps on the page. For additional practice, make sure students switch roles (Student A becomes Student B and vice versa) and repeat Steps 2 and 3. When all students have completed all parts of both pages, check everyone's work, or have students check their own or each others' work.

Evaluation

To use the Check Your Competency pages successfully, follow these suggested procedures.

Before and during each evaluation, create a relaxed, affirming atmosphere. Chat with the students for a few minutes and review the material. When you and the students are ready, have students read the directions and look over each exercise before they complete it. If at any time you sense that students are becoming frustrated, stop to provide additional review. Resume when students are ready. The evaluation formats follow two basic patterns:

1. Speaking competencies are checked in the same two-part format used to present them in the unit. In the first part, a review, students fill in missing words in a brief conversation. In the second part, marked with the *Check Up*

symbol, students' ability to use the competency is checked. Students use the dialog they have just completed as a model for their own conversations. As in the rest of the unit, color indicates the words students change to talk about themselves. Follow these suggestions:

♦ When students are ready, have them complete the written portion. Check their answers. Then have students practice the dialog in pairs.

♦ Continue with the spoken part of the evaluation. Make sure that students remember that they are to substitute words about themselves for the words in color. Have students complete the spoken part in any or all of these ways:

Self- and Peer Evaluation: Have students complete the spoken activity in pairs. Students in each pair evaluate themselves and/or each other and report the results to you.

Teacher/Pair Evaluation: Have pairs complete the activity as you observe. Begin with the most proficient students. As other students who are ready to be evaluated wait, have them practice in pairs. Students who complete the evaluation successfully can peer-teach those who are waiting or those who need additional review.

Teacher/Individual Evaluation: Have individuals complete the activity with you as partner. Follow the procedures in Teacher/Pair Evaluation.

2. Listening, reading, and **writing** competencies are checked in a simple one-step process. When students are ready to begin, have them read the instructions. Demonstrate the first item and have students complete the activity. Then check their work. If necessary, provide any review needed, and have students try the activity again.

When students demonstrate mastery of a competency to your satisfaction, have them record their success by checking the appropriate box at the top of their Student Book page. The Teacher's Edition also contains charts for you to reproduce and use to keep track of individual and class progress.

Real-Life English

Personal Communication

Where are the people? What are they doing? What do you think?

Listen and practice the dialogs.

A.
➤ Would you like to have lunch together on Friday?
● That sounds great.

B.
➤ Let's go bowling.
● I'd rather stay home.

C.
➤ How about dinner tonight?
● I'm sorry. Thanh and I have already made other plans.

D.
➤ Would you like to go to a movie tomorrow night?
● Sure. What time do you want to go?
➤ How about 7:30?

Starting Out

 A. Look at the dialogs on page 2 and the pictures on this page. Match. Write the letters in the boxes.

1. Marta and Mel are in the same English class. Marta wants to invite Mel to go to a movie.

2. Son and Lisa are married. They're making plans for this evening.

3. Menh and Vantha are friends. Menh is inviting Vantha and his roommate for dinner.

4. Yoshi and Tom work together. Tom wants to invite Yoshi to lunch on Friday.

B. Answer the questions.

1. Who accepted the invitations? Who turned down the invitations?
2. Which invitations would you accept? Why?

 C. Work with a partner. Invite your partner to do something.

Talk It Over

A. Practice the dialog.

> ➤ Let's go out for pizza after work sometime this week.
> ● OK. When?
> ➤ Is **Wednesday** good for you, **Melissa?**
> ● **That sounds like** a good idea. How about you, **John?**
> ■ I can't. I have **to go to the dentist at 5:30.**
> ● What about **Thursday at 5:30?**
> ■ That's fine with me.

B. Fill in the date book.
Write what you are doing each day.

	Morning	Afternoon	Evening
Thursday			
Friday			
Saturday			

C. Work with a small group.
Use the dialog in A to set a time to go out for pizza.
Use your date book to ask and answer questions.

Word Bank

A. Study the vocabulary.

Social Activities	Feelings	
bowling	angry	*Useful Language*
concert	confused	That sounds good/nice/great.
game	happy	That sounds like a good/great idea.
party	hurt	Sure.
picnic	shy	I'm sorry. I'm busy (tonight).
	surprised	Maybe some other time.
	terrible	Sorry. I've got other plans.
accept	upset	RSVP
turn down		

**B. When English speakers turn down an invitation, they usually give a reason.
Work with a partner. Practice the dialog.**

➤ Would you like to go to **a movie tonight?**
● I'm sorry. I'm **busy tonight. I have to work.**
➤ How about another time?
● That sounds good. Let's go **on Friday.**
➤ OK.

C. Write more good reasons for turning down an invitation.

1. I'm not feeling very well.

2. _____

3. _____

4. _____

D. Invite your partner to do something. Listen to your partner's invitation. Turn it down.

Listening

A. Look and listen. Who did Bob talk to?
   Circle the letter of the correct picture.

1.

   (a.)   b.

2.

   a.   b.

3.

   a.   b.

B. Listen again. What's the relationship of each person to Bob? Write the answer in column A.

	A	B	C
1.	mother	lunch	(yes) no don't know
2.	_____	_____	yes no don't know
3.	_____	_____	yes no don't know

Listen again. Write what the invitation is for in column B.

Listen again. Did the person accept the invitation? Circle the answer in column C.

Reading

A. Look and read.

DEAR ELLEN

DEAR ELLEN: I have a problem that upsets me very much. I have worried so much about this that I decided to write for advice. I'm from Greece, and I teach a class in Greek cooking at the adult school. My American students are very friendly. I have given them my address and have invited them to drop by to see me, but no one has ever come. Recently one of my students told me to drop by and see her. I went to visit her yesterday. She seemed very surprised to see me. She talked to me in the doorway. She didn't even invite me inside! I felt terrible. Why do Americans say things they don't mean?

—Confused

DEAR CONFUSED: Americans very often say "Drop by" or "Come by some time" to show that they have friendly feelings. The words usually are not a real invitation. Americans usually call on the telephone before they visit instead of just "dropping by." That gives the person enough time to get ready for the visit. Why don't you invite one of your students to do something on a day that you both choose? Go to a movie, have lunch, or visit in your home. I think you'll be very pleasantly surprised!

B. Look and read. Write *yes* or *no*.

1. Confused is upset because she invited students to drop by for a visit, and they didn't come.   _yes_

2. The students in the cooking class are unfriendly.   _____

3. An invitation to drop by is a real invitation.   _____

4. Americans usually call on the telephone before they visit.   _____

5. Ellen tells Confused to stop inviting students to visit.   _____

C. Work with a group. Discuss the questions.

1. Do you agree with the advice? Why or why not?
2. What advice would you give Confused?
3. Have you ever had a problem like this? How did you feel?

Structure Base

A. Study the examples.

> | I'm | late for work. |
> | He's | |
> | They're | |

B. Complete the sentences. Follow the examples in A.

➤ Hi, Mel. It's Lupe. _____Are_____ you and your roommate ready to go to the movies?

● _____ ready, but my roommate Ken isn't.

_____ a little late.

➤ _____ ready to go now. Do you want me to give you both a ride?

● That's a good idea. Do you need to pick up Rob and Suzanne, also?

➤ No. _____ already at the theater. I'll be at your house in about 10 minutes.

C. Study the examples.

> He makes plans for lunch every day.
> He's making plans for lunch right now.
> He's already made plans for lunch.

D. Complete the sentences. Use the correct form of the word.

1. Alma _____likes_____ (like) to go to the movies.

2. Binh _____ (enjoy) movies, too.

3. Right now she_____ (ask) him to join her.

4. Alma_____ already _____ (decide) which movie she wants to see.

E. Study the examples.

She feels	happy. sad. angry. disappointed. confused. hurt. shy. surprised. upset. good.

F. Complete the sentences. Use the words in E.

1. Lupe loves music, but she can't go to the concert today.

   She probably feels _____.

2. Chan enjoys bowling. His friends asked him to go bowling.

   He felt _____.

3. I always invite Bill to my parties. I didn't get an invitation to

   Bill's party. I feel _____.

G. Work with a partner. Find out how your partner felt.

1. You got a good grade on the test. How did you feel?

   _____

2. You went to a party last weekend. How did you feel?

   _____

3. Your friend had a car accident. How did you feel?

   _____

4. You went to a movie. The movie was terrible. How did you feel?

   _____

Write It Down

A. Look and read. Complete the invitation. Use the information.

Laura and Miguel Mercado are having an open house on April 7. Their address is 3902 Oak Avenue. The party is from 4:00 to 7:00 P.M.

COME TO AN OPEN HOUSE

Date: _____APRIL 7_____

Time: _____

Place: _____

Given By: _____

RSVP: _____555-3267._____

About You

B. You're having a party at your house. Choose a time and a date. Complete the invitation.

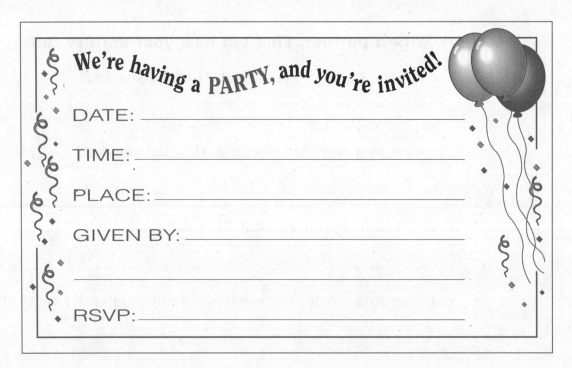

We're having a PARTY, and you're invited!

DATE: _____

TIME: _____

PLACE: _____

GIVEN BY: _____

_____

RSVP: _____

I. Practice the dialog.

➤ Would you like to go to a **movie?**

● When?

➤ Thursday at 8:30.

● I'm sorry. I'm busy on Thursday night. I'm going to a concert with my mom. Thanks for the invitation, though.

2. Use the dialog in I.
Invite Student B to each activity.
Can Student B go? Circle *yes* or *no*.

a. a movie on Thursday at 8:30 P.M.   yes (no)

b. dinner and a movie Friday at 6:00 P.M.   yes   no

c. a picnic on Saturday from 12:30 P.M. to 3:00 P.M.   yes   no

d. a concert on Sunday at 4:00 P.M.   yes   no

3. Listen to Student B's invitations.
Look at your date book.
If you can go, write the activity and time in your book.

Thursday	Friday	Saturday	Sunday
Work 6-3	Work 6-3	Work 6-12	
		Picnic 12:30 to 3:00 P.M.	
Movie 8:30 P.M.	Go out to dinner and movie at 6:00 P.M.		Concert 4:00 P.M.

4. Switch roles. Turn to page 12. Complete 2 and 3.

l. Practice the dialog.

➤ Would you like to go to a **movie?**

● When?

➤ Thursday at 8:30.

● I'm sorry. I'm busy on Thursday night. I'm going to a concert with my mom. Thanks for the invitation, though.

2. Listen to Student A's invitations.
Look at your date book.
If you can go, write the activity and time in your book.

Thursday	Friday	Saturday	Sunday
Work 7-3	Interview for new job 11:30 A.M.	Work 7-3	Walk in the park 10:00 A.M.
	Lunch 12:30 P.M.		
Dentist 4:00 P.M. Pizza Dinner 5:30 P.M.		Bowling 4:00 P.M.	Birthday Party for Mom, 7:00 P.M.
Concert with Mom 8:30 P.M.			

3. Use the dialog in l.
Invite Student A to each activity.
Can Student A go? Circle *yes* or *no*.

a. a pizza dinner on Thursday at 5:30 P.M.   (yes)   no

b. lunch on Friday at 12:30 P.M.   yes   no

c. bowling on Saturday at 4:00 P.M.   yes   no

d. a walk in the park on Sunday at 10:00 A.M.   yes   no

4. Switch roles. Turn to page ll. Complete 2 and 3.

Extension

A. You went to an open house at Mr. and Mrs. Mercado's house. You had a wonderful time. You enjoyed meeting their friends. You sent them a thank-you note. Complete the thank-you note.

✔

| open house   wonderful   inviting   enjoyed |

Dear Mr. and Mrs. Mercado,

    Thank you for ___inviting___ me to your

_____ . I had a _____ time.

I really _____ meeting all your family and your friends.

                  Best wishes,

                 _____

About You

B. Imagine you went to a party at Mr. and Mrs. Lee's house. You had fun. The food was delicious. Write a thank-you note.

Can you use the competencies?

☐ 1. Offer invitations
☐ 2. Accept invitations
☐ 3. Turn down invitations
☐ 4. Write invitations

A. Review competencies 1 and 2.
Complete the dialog.

✔

| How about   on Saturday   Would you   Sounds great   What time |

➤ <u>Would you</u> _____ like to come over for lunch on Saturday?

● Sure. _____?

➤ _____ 12:30?

● _____. I'll be there.

➤ I'll see you _____.

Check Up

Use competencies 1 and 2.
Work with a partner. Give and accept invitations
to go to two of the places.

1. to a movie tomorrow night
2. to a dinner next Saturday
3. to a birthday party Friday night

B. Review competency 3. Complete the dialog.

✔

| sorry   have other plans   inviting me   some other time |

➤ Would you like to go to the game on Thursday?

● I'm ___<u>sorry</u>___, but I _____. Thanks for

_____. Maybe we can go _____.

➤ OK. I'll call you next week.

Use competency 3. Work with a partner.
Give and turn down invitations to go to two of the places.

1. to a concert next Thursday
2. to dinner tonight
3. to a baseball game on Tuesday night

C. Use competency 4.
You are inviting friends over for dinner at your house.
Complete the invitation.

A DINNER PARTY

DATE: _____

TIME: _____

PLACE: _____

GIVEN BY: _____

RSVP: _____

2 Our Community

Where are the people? What are they doing? What do you think?

Read the story.

Nina Ramos used to cash her paychecks at the grocery store every Saturday. But one day a man's wallet was stolen while he was leaving the store. So now Nina takes her paycheck to the bank. She deposits most of her paycheck in her checking account and gets only a little cash. At the grocery store she pays for her groceries by check.

Starting Out

A. Look and read.

1. Last Saturday Nina Ramos went to the bank to deposit her paycheck. The teller was helping another customer when she arrived.

2. Nina turned the check over and signed her name. While she was endorsing her check, the teller asked her for the deposit slip and her ID.

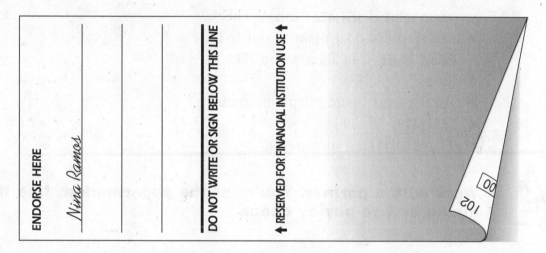

3. The bank teller checked Nina's signature and ID. He added the deposit to her checking account, and handed her the rest in cash.

B. Study Nina's check. You want to deposit a check. Endorse it.

ENDORSE HERE

_____

_____

DO NOT WRITE OR SIGN BELOW THIS LINE

Talk It Over

 A. Nina is paying for her groceries. Practice the dialog.

➤ Your total is **$51.47.** Cash or check?
● Check. Who do I make it out to?
➤ **Food Mart.** Can I see some ID?
● Sure.
➤ What's your home telephone number?
● **555-1429.**
➤ Thanks. Have a nice day!

 B. Work with a partner. You're at the supermarket. Use the dialog in A to pay by check.

C. Talk to three students. Ask them the questions. Write *check* or *cash* to complete the chart.

Name	How do you pay for your groceries?	How do you pay your rent?	How do you pay your utilities?
Nina	check	check	check

Word Bank

DEPOSIT TICKET

Name _Lisa Hardin_

Address _795 Oak Street Apt. 12_

San Francisco, CA 97590

Date _October 4_ 19 _95_

DEPOSITS MAY NOT BE AVAILABLE FOR IMMEDIATE WITHDRAWAL

Lisa Hardin

SIGN HERE FOR CASH RECEIVED IF REQUIRED

THRIFTY BANK
San Francisco, CA 90211

⑆11492127⑆9949⑈094977331⑆0⑈

CASH	Currency		
	Coin		
LIST CHECKS SINGLY		175	00
		142	00
Total From Other Side			
TOTAL		317	00
Less Cash Received		35	00
NET DEPOSIT		282	00

A. Study the vocabulary.

balance

bounce a check

cash

checkbook

checkbook
  register

checking account

deposit slip

endorse

ID

paycheck

steal

utilities

> ***Useful Language***
>
> Can I see some ID?
>
> Who do I make it out to?

 B. You have two checks to deposit.
One is for $150 and one is for $20.
Fill out the deposit slip. Get $10 in cash.

DEPOSIT TICKET

Name _____

Address _____

_____

Date _____ 19 _____

DEPOSITS MAY NOT BE AVAILABLE FOR IMMEDIATE WITHDRAWAL

SIGN HERE FOR CASH RECEIVED IF REQUIRED

THRIFTY BANK
San Francisco, CA 90211

⑆11492127⑆9949⑈094977331⑆0⑈

CASH	Currency		
	Coin		
LIST CHECKS SINGLY		150	00
Total From Other Side			
TOTAL			
Less Cash Received			
NET DEPOSIT			

Listening

A. Look and listen. What are they doing?
Circle the answers in Column A.

	A		**B**	
1.	(buying groceries)	buying clothes	(cash)	check
2.	paying the electric bill	paying the rent	cash	check
3.	paying the gas bill	paying the rent	cash	check

Listen again. How did they pay?
Circle the answers in Column B.

B. Look and listen. Answer the questions. Write _yes_ or _no_.

1. Does the Super Service Account include both
   checking and savings?   _yes_

2. Are all the services for the Super Service
   Account free?   _____

3. Can you get customer service 24 hours a day?   _____

Look and listen again. What are the bank charges?
Write the amounts.

1. You pay a ___$5.00___ monthly service charge.

2. If you keep _____ in your account, you pay no fee.

3. You can get _____ money orders a month at no charge.

C. What do you think of the Super Service Account?
Would you want it? Why or why not? Write two sentences.

_____

_____

Reading

A. **You've called several banks for information about services and charges. Look at your notes.**

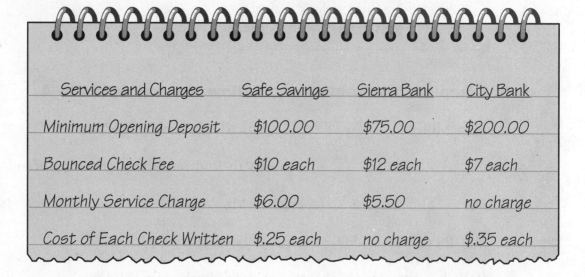

Services and Charges	Safe Savings	Sierra Bank	City Bank
Minimum Opening Deposit	$100.00	$75.00	$200.00
Bounced Check Fee	$10 each	$12 each	$7 each
Monthly Service Charge	$6.00	$5.50	no charge
Cost of Each Check Written	$.25 each	no charge	$.35 each

B. **Answer the questions. Use the information in A.**

1. Joe started a new job. He has $75 from his first paycheck to put into a checking account. At which bank can he open an account?

   <u>Sierra Bank</u>

2. Tim often makes mistakes in his checkbook. Sometimes he writes checks when he doesn't have enough money in his account. The checks bounce. Which bank should Tim choose?

   _____

3. Elsa writes only five or six checks each month. She usually pays cash. Should she choose Safe Savings or City Bank?

   _____

4. Sylvia writes about forty checks each month. Which bank should she choose for her checking account?

   _____

C. **Work with your partner.**
Which bank would you choose? Why?

Structure Base

A. Study the examples.

She	deposited a check yesterday.
They	went to the bank on Monday.

B. Complete the sentences. Follow the examples in A.

Mrs. Miller _____went_____ (go) to the bank yesterday. She

_____ (want) to find out about checking accounts.

She _____ (speak) to Mr. Vega. He _____ (say)

that there was a $5.00 monthly service charge. He _____

(tell) her there is no charge for each check. Mrs. Miller

_____ (open) an account at the bank.

C. When did you go to the bank?
What did you do there? Follow the sentences in B.

D. Study the examples.

She was opening an account when I arrived at the bank.
When I arrived at the bank, she was opening an account.

Ahmed deposited the check while I was waiting in the car.
While I was waiting in the car, Ahmed deposited the check.

E. Complete the sentences. Follow the examples in D.

1. Don and Lee _____were opening_____ (open) an account when I saw them at the bank.

2. When I ran into Ahmed, he _____ (talk) to the bank teller.

3. Nina _____ (endorse) her check while she was waiting in line.

4. While Lee was watching the children, I _____ (deposit) my paycheck.

5. I deposited my check while my wife _____ (wait) in the car.

F. Study the examples.

> Did she use to cash her checks at the supermarket?

I	used to cash checks at the supermarket.
You	
He	
She	
We	
They	

G. Read the sentences. Circle the correct answer.
Follow the examples in F.

1. Nina (used to cash) / cashes her checks at the grocery store. Now she used to deposit / **deposits** them at the bank.

2. Nina now **used to pay / pays** for her groceries by check.

3. Nina **used to carry / carries** cash with her all the time. Now she **writes / used to write** checks.

H. How did you use to pay your bills in your country?
How do you pay them now?

Write It Down

A. **You should write all your checks, deposits, service charges, and withdrawals in your checkbook register. If you don't, you won't know how much money you have. Look and read.**

		RECORD ALL TRANSACTIONS THAT AFFECT YOUR ACCOUNT					BALANCE	
NUMBER	DATE	DESCRIPTION OF TRANSACTION	PAYMENT (−)		DEPOSIT (+)		500	00
101	4/2	Pay credit card	120	00			-120	00
							380	00
	4/8	Paycheck			525	00	+525	00
							905	00
102	4/11	Sam's Market	25	00			-25	00

What's the balance? ___$905.00___

B. **Write the items in the checkbook register.**
   Add deposits. Subtract checks you wrote and bank charges.

1. You wrote check 102 on April 11 to Sam's Market.
   The amount was $25.00.
2. On April 25, you deposited your tax refund. The amount was $120.00.
3. On April 28, you wrote check 103 to City Gas Company.
   The amount was $20.00.
4. On April 30, the bank took out its monthly service charge of $8.00.

What's the final balance? _____

I. **A customer wants information about checking accounts at Town Savings. Practice the dialog.**

➤ What's the minimum opening deposit?

● It's $100.00.

2. **You want to open an account at Town Savings. Follow the dialog in I. Ask Student B about the charges. Write the answers.**

TOWN SAVINGS

Service	Charge
Minimum opening deposit	$100.00
Bounced check fee	
Monthly service charge	
Cost of each check written	

3. **You work at First Bank and Trust. Answer Student B's questions about the charges.**

◁ FIRST BANK AND TRUST ▷

Service	Charge
Minimum opening deposit	$75.00
Bounced check fee	$10.00 each
Monthly service charge	$ 5.00
Cost of each check written	$ .15 each

4. **Switch roles. Turn to page 26. Complete 2 and 3.**

5. **Where do you want to open an account, First Bank and Trust or Town Savings? Why?**

1. **A customer wants information about checking accounts at Town Savings. Practice the dialog.**

   ➤ What's the minimum opening deposit?
   ● It's **$100.00.**

2. **You work at Town Savings. Answer Student A's questions about the charges.**

   ## TOWN SAVINGS

Service	Charge
Minimum opening deposit	$100.00
Bounced check fee	$ 12.00 each
Monthly service charge	$ 8.00
Cost of each check written	$ .25 each

3. **You want to open an account at First Bank and Trust. Follow the dialog in I. Ask Student A about the charges. Write the answers.**

   ### FIRST BANK AND TRUST

Service	Charge
Minimum opening deposit	$75.00
Bounced check fee	
Monthly service charge	
Cost of each check written	

4. **Switch roles. Turn to page 25. Complete 2 and 3.**

5. **Where do you want to open an account, First Bank and Trust or Town Savings? Why?**

Extension

A. Look and read.

ATMs MAKE BANKING EASIER

Many banks offer ATM services to their customers. (ATM stands for "Automatic Teller Machine.") The ATM is connected to the bank's computer. You can do many bank transactions at an ATM, such as depositing or withdrawing money from your checking or savings account and finding out your account balance.

Easy steps for any transaction

To use the ATM, you must get a special card and a secret ID code from the bank. You use the card and code for all transactions. For example, you must follow these steps at the ATM when you want to take out money:

1. Insert your card.
2. Enter your ID number.
3. Press buttons indicating the transaction.
4. Take your cash from the machine.
5. Punch a button indicating the end of the transaction.
6. Get back your card.
7. Take your receipt from the machine.

Be safe at the ATM

Follow safety precautions when using an ATM. Don't give your card or code to anyone. Don't write your ID number on your card. And be very careful when you are at the machine, especially at night.

B. Work with a partner. Answer the questions.

1. How do you use an ATM?
2. Are ATMs easy to use? Why or why not?
3. Are ATMs safe? What do you think?
4. Do you have an ATM card? Why or why not?

Can you use the competencies?

☐ 1. Endorse checks
☐ 2. Pay by check
☐ 3. Compare bank services
☐ 4. Balance checkbooks

A. Use competency I. Endorse the check.

ENDORSE HERE

DO NOT WRITE OR SIGN BELOW THIS LINE

B. Review competency 2. Complete the dialog. ✔

| ID   telephone number   check   make it out to |

➤ Your total is $62.35. Cash or check?

● Check_____.Who do I _____?

➤ Foodland. Can I see your _____?

● Sure.

➤ What's your home _____?

● 555-8094.

➤ Thanks.

Use competency 2. Follow the dialog above to pay for your groceries by check.

C. Use competency 3. Which account do you want? Why?

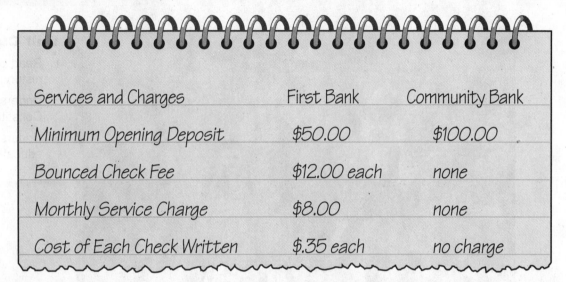

Services and Charges	First Bank	Community Bank
Minimum Opening Deposit	$50.00	$100.00
Bounced Check Fee	$12.00 each	none
Monthly Service Charge	$8.00	none
Cost of Each Check Written	$.35 each	no charge

D. Use competency 4. Write the items in the checkbook register. Add deposits. Subtract checks and bank charges.

1. You wrote check 103 on May 1 to pay the rent. The amount was $400.00.
2. On May 6, you deposited your paycheck. The amount was $525.75.
3. You wrote check 104 on May 16 to Food Mart. The amount was $33.00.
4. On May 18, you deposited a check you received for your birthday. The amount was $25.00.
5. On May 20, the bank took out its monthly service charge of $5.00.

What's the final balance? _____

		RECORD ALL TRANSACTIONS THAT AFFECT YOUR ACCOUNT					
NUMBER	DATE	DESCRIPTION OF TRANSACTION	PAYMENT OR FEE(−)		DEPOSIT (+)	**BALANCE** 630	00
103	5/1	Rent	400	00		−400	00

3 Our Country

Unit Competencies

1. Read about U.S. history
2. Understand the U.S. Constitution
3. Understand equal educational opportunity

Who are the people? What are they doing? What do you think?

Read the article.

The U.S. is a nation of many different people and cultures. Thousands of years ago, the ancestors of today's Native Americans arrived in America. They probably came from Asia. Then in the 1500s and 1600s Spanish, English, and French explorers and settlers arrived. During the 1800s and early 1900s, millions of people from Europe and Asia came here to live.

Immigrants have come to America from all over the world. They have come for many different reasons. Almost all have come hoping to make better lives for themselves and their families.

Starting Out

A. Look and read.

1. The first people to arrive in America were the ancestors of today's Native Americans. They were probably looking for food.

2. Starting in the 1500s, the Spanish explored and settled in what are now the southeastern and western parts of the U.S.

3. The first permanent settlers from England began arriving in the 1600s. The Pilgrims, for example, came here in 1620 looking for religious freedom. They settled in Massachusetts.

4. Immigrants continue to come here from Mexico, Central and South America, Europe, Asia, and almost every other part of the world.

B. Answer the questions.

1. Who explored the southeastern and western parts of the U.S.?
2. Where do today's immigrants come from?

Talk It Over

 A. Harry is asking Ming Chin about coming to the U.S. Practice the dialog.

➤ When did you come here?

● **About three years ago.**

➤ Why did you decide to come here?

● **Mainly for political freedom. People can't always say what they think in China.**

➤ Do you have any relatives here in the U.S.?

● **Yes, my brother. I'm very glad he came with me.**

B. Talk to four students. Ask them the questions. Write the answers. Use the dialog in A.

Name	Where is your family from?	When did you come here?	Why did you come here?
Ming Chin	China	three years ago	political freedom

Word Bank

A. Study the vocabulary.

amendment	immigrate	religious freedom
the Bill of Rights	liberty	rights
explorer	Native American	settler
guarantees	Pilgrim	the U.S. Constitution
immigrant	political freedom	

B. Where did they come from? Match.

_b_ 1. Spaniards   a. Asia

____ 2. Native Americans   b. Spain

____ 3. Pilgrims   c. England

C. Work with a small group.
Use the map to show where you are from.

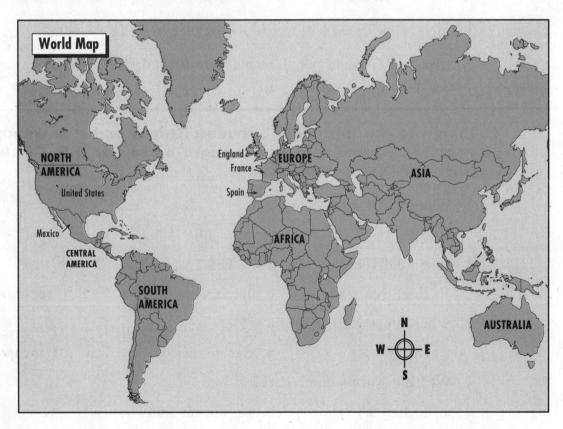

Listening

A. Look and listen. When did they come here? Show the order. Write the numbers from 1 to 5.

_____ Africans

_____ Spaniards

  1   Native Americans

_____ Pilgrims

_____ Chinese, Irish, and Germans

Listen again. Why did they come here? Write _yes_ or _no_.

1. The ancestors of today's Native Americans probably came here from Asia to look for food.   _yes_

2. The Spanish explorers came here for religious freedom. _____

3. The Pilgrims came here because they wanted to find gold. _____

4. The Africans were forced to come here to work as slaves. _____

5. Irish and German people came here to find food, work, and political freedom. _____

B. Listen to the interview between Karma and a newspaper reporter. Karma recently immigrated to the U.S. Circle the letter of the correct answer.

1. Where did Karma come from?

   (a.) Tibet   b. Mongolia   c. Nepal

2. When did Karma come to the U.S.?

   a. three years ago   b. three weeks ago   c. three months ago

3. Where does Karma live now?

   a. Miami   b. San Francisco   c. Minneapolis

4. Why did Karma come here?

   a. to find a job   b. to join his family

   c. for political freedom

Reading

A. Look and read.

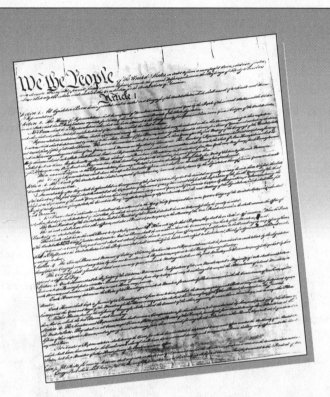

Immigrants have come to the U.S. for many reasons. One of the most important reasons people come here is for political freedom.

The U.S. Constitution and its amendments guarantee certain rights and freedoms. Many of these rights are guaranteed by the first ten amendments of the constitution. For this reason, these amendments are called the **Bill of Rights.** Three of these rights are freedom of speech, press, and religion. Other important amendments ended slavery, gave men of all races the right to vote, and gave women the right to vote.

All U.S. citizens have certain rights because they are citizens. These rights are called **civil rights.** In addition to constitutional amendments, many court decisions have been made to help guarantee the civil rights of all U.S. citizens. Court decisions have helped integrate the public schools, give access to public buildings to people with disabilities, and make it easier for all U.S. citizens to vote.

B. Answer the questions.

1. What are the first ten amendments of the U.S. Constitution called?
2. What are three rights guaranteed by the Bill of Rights?
3. What are civil rights?

Structure Base

A. Study the examples.

| He arrived in the U.S. | two years three weeks | ago. |

B. Read the questions. Write the answers.
Tell about Lech's life before 1994. Follow the examples in A.

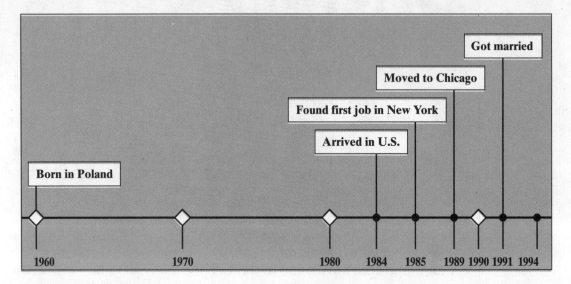

1. When was Lech born?

   _____

2. When did he come to the U.S.?

   _____

3. When did he find his first job?

   _____

4. When did he move to Chicago?

   _____

5. When did he get married?

   _____

C. Work with a partner.
Tell about your life in the U.S. Follow the sentences in B.

D. Study the examples.

> How long has she lived in Miami?

She's lived in Miami since	1963. March.

She's lived in Miami for	thirty years. six months.

E. Complete the sentences. Circle *for* or *since*.

1. I have worked at the Johnson Company **(for)** / **since** thirteen years.

2. I have known him **for** / **since** 1983.

3. My brother has lived in the U.S. **for** / **since** three years.

4. They have not visited their family in Russia **for** / **since** 1984.

5. Tom has been in California **for** / **since** four days.

F. Work with a partner. Answer the questions.
Talk about Jean's life. Follow the examples in D.

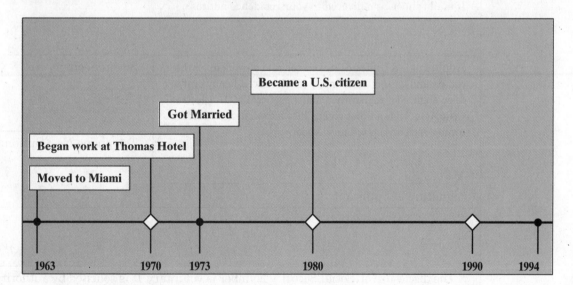

1. How long has Jean lived in Miami?
2. How long has Jean worked at the Thomas Hotel?
3. How long has Jean been married?
4. How long has Jean been a U.S. citizen?

Write It Down

Look and read.

Every U.S. citizen has the right to vote.
Complete the Voter Registration Application.
Use information about yourself or someone you know.

VOTER REGISTRATION APPLICATION
PLEASE COMPLETE ALL OF THE INFORMATION. PRINT IN INK OR TYPE.

Last Name	First Name (NOT HUSBAND'S)	Middle Name (If any)

Sex	Date of Birth: month, day, year	Place of Birth: city or county, state or foreign country

Residence Address: Street Address and Apartment Number, City, State, and ZIP.
If none, describe location of residence.

Mailing Address, City, State, and ZIP.
If mail cannot be delivered to your residence address.

Applicant is a United States citizen and a resident of the county and has not been finally convicted of a felony or if a felon eligible for registration under section 13.001, Election Code. I understand that giving false information to procure a voter registration is a misdemeanor.	Social Security No.*
X _____ Signature of Applicant	Telephone No. (Optional)

Court of Naturalization, If applicable

* The disclosure of Social Security Number is voluntary. It is solicited by authority of sec. 13.122 and will be used only to maintain the accuracy of the registration records.

I. Two friends are talking about a new neighbor. Practice the dialog.

➤ Where is **Mandisa** from?

● He's from **Zaire.**

➤ When did he come to the U.S.?

● He arrived **about three years ago.**

➤ Why did he come to the U.S.?

● **He wanted to find a good job so he could help support his family.**

2. Ask Student B about Bao. Follow the dialog in I. Write the answers.

Where?	When?	Why?

3. Read about Ivana. Answer Student B's questions. Follow the dialog in I.

Ivana came to the U.S. from Russia in 1989. In Russia Ivana worked in a government factory, but the factory closed. It was very difficult for her to find a new job, so Ivana came here to look for work. In 1990, Ivana's parents and her brother came to join her in the U.S.

4. Switch roles. Turn to page 40. Complete 2 and 3.

**I. Two friends are talking about a new neighbor.
Practice the dialog.**

> ➤ Where is **Mandisa** from?
> ● He's from **Zaire.**
> ➤ When did he come to the U.S.?
> ● He arrived **about three years ago.**
> ➤ Why did he come to the U.S.?
> ● He wanted to find a good job so he could help support his family.

**2. Read about Bao. Answer Student A's questions.
Follow the dialog in I.**

In 1972 Bao and his brothers arrived in Los Angeles, California. They left
Vietnam and came to the U.S. to join their mother. It was too dangerous
to stay in Vietnam because of the war.

**3. Ask Student A about Ivana. Follow the dialog in I.
Write the answers.**

Where?	When?	Why?

4. Switch roles. Turn to page 39. Complete 2 and 3.

Extension

A. Read.

All people in the U.S. have certain rights. One of these is the right to a free public education for all children. In 1982 the Supreme Court decided that this includes the children of undocumented aliens. The court said that *all children have the right to a free public education, even if their parents do not have proper documentation.* The Supreme Court decision *(Plyler* vs. *Doe)* guarantees this right to every child living in the U.S.

B. Read the sentences. Write *yes* or *no.*

1. Parents need proper documentation before their children can go to school.   no
2. In 1982 the Supreme Court decided that all children have the right to a free public education. _____
3. The Supreme Court decision applies to children living outside of the U.S. _____

Can you use the competencies?

☐ 1. Read about U.S. history
☐ 2. Understand the U.S. Constitution
☐ 3. Understand equal educational opportunity

A. Review competency I. Look and read.

Thousands of years ago, people started coming to the Americas to live. Native Americans were living here long before Spanish explorers arrived in the 1550s and 1600s. The Pilgrims came looking for religious freedom in the 1600s. In the 1600s Africans were brought here to work as slaves. During the 1800s and 1900s, millions of immigrants from all over the world entered the U.S.

Some people have come to the U.S. because they want political and religious freedom. Others have come here because of wars, hunger, or poverty in their countries. And still others are looking for better jobs. Most people come to the U.S. looking for better lives.

Check Up

Use competency I. Write *yes* or *no.*

1. The Pilgrims arrived here before the Spanish explorers.   no

2. Africans began arriving in this country in the 1400s.   _____

3. Some people come to the U.S. to find political and religious freedom.   _____

4. Wars, poverty, and hunger cause some people to leave their native countries.   _____

B. Use competency 2. Match the word and the definition. Write the letter of the correct definition.

<u>a</u>   1. the U.S. Constitution

_____ 2. civil rights

_____ 3. the Bill of Rights

_____ 4. amendment

✔a. the document that guarantees all U.S. citizens certain rights

b. the first ten amendments to the U.S. Constitution

c. the rights guaranteed by the U.S. Constitution

d. a change made to the U.S. Constitution

C. Use competency 3.
Read the questions. Circle the answers.

1. Do all children in the U.S. have a right to a free public education?

        (yes)   no

2. Did the Supreme Court decide that all children in the U.S. can attend public schools?

        yes   no

3. Do parents have to be U.S. citizens for their children to go to public schools?

        yes   no

4 Daily Living

Where are the people? What are they doing? What do you think?

Read the story.

Thun moved to the city last month. She likes living close to work. Before she moved, she had to get up early and take the bus to work. She used to spend a lot of time in traffic. Now she can walk to work or ride her bicycle. She can also walk or ride to the grocery store, which is located on the corner, next to the park.

There are some problems, though. Thun doesn't like the noise pollution or the litter in the streets. To get away from these things, she sometimes goes to the library or out to the country for an afternoon. Crime also worries Thun. To make sure she's safe, she always locks her windows and doors.

Starting Out

A. Look and read.

1. Many people are affected by smog and other air pollution. Breathing dirty air can be bad for your health.

2. Crime is a problem in a lot of communities. Some people install extra locks to discourage burglars from breaking in.

3. Noise pollution is a problem in many areas. Loud noises from jets, for example, can damage hearing.

4. Litter is a problem almost everywhere. People can help keep their communities clean by throwing garbage into trash cans.

About You

B. Work with a partner. Answer the questions.

1. Does your community have any of these problems? Which ones?

2. Do any of these problems affect you? Which ones?

Talk It Over

 A. Peter is telling his sister about living in the city. Practice the dialog.

➤ How do you like living here, **Peter?**

● It's **OK, but the traffic is awful.**

➤ What do you mean?

● **The freeways are jammed. I spend a lot of time every day just going to and from work.**

➤ **Maybe you should start taking the subway to work, like I do.**

● **That's a good idea.**

 B. Use the dialog in A. Talk to four students about where they live. What are the problems? How can they be solved? Complete the chart.

Name	Problem	Solution
Peter	traffic	take the subway

Word Bank

A. Study the vocabulary.

Problems	Solutions
burglars	lock
crime	recycling
jammed	
litter	affected by
noise	environment
pollution	get away from
smog	look forward to
traffic	pulled out
trash	

RECYCLING SYMBOL

B. Talk to four students.
What are some good things about living in a city?
What are some bad things? Complete the chart.

THE CITY	
Good Things	**Bad Things**
exciting	a lot of traffic

C. Work with a partner.
Talk about your experiences living in the city or in the country.

Listening

A. A community action group is having a meeting to talk about some of the problems in Northridge. Look and listen. Write the solution to each problem

1. crime

   _____ add more streetlights and police _____

2. trash in parks

   _____

3. noise

   _____

Listen again. Which problem has not been solved? Circle the answer.

crime   trash in parks   smog

B. Some friends are talking about problems in the city. What's the problem? Write the answer in column A.

A		B
1. ____crime____	You can buy an alarm.	You can use public transportation.
2. _____	You can lock your door.	You can write to an official.
3. _____	You can exercise.	You can go out only when necessary.

Listen again.
Circle what can be done in column B.

Reading

A. Look and read.

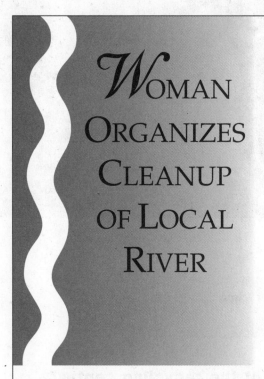

WOMAN ORGANIZES CLEANUP OF LOCAL RIVER

The Housatonic River runs through the town of Great Barrington, Massachusetts. Like many other rivers, the banks of the Housatonic River had become littered with trash. There were trees damaged by storms, the remains of burned buildings, and household trash strewn along the river's banks.

In March, 1988, Rachel Field noticed how littered the river banks had become. She began to organize a group of volunteers to clean up the trash. She talked to her friends and co-workers, and she was able to get enough volunteers to clean a 40-foot section of the river bank. The volunteers then planted grass on the land they had cleared.

Two years later, Rachel Field organized a second cleanup. One section of the river bank was covered with debris from a drug store that had burned down many years before. Rachel convinced the owner of the drug store to allow them to remove all the trash. Dozens of volunteers formed a line to move trash, one piece at a time, from the lower part of the river bank up to a dumpster on the road. Thousands of pounds of trash were removed.

The work of Rachel Field and the volunteers was appreciated by the town of Great Barrington. In 1990 the Rotary Club named Rachel Field Citizen of the Year.◆

B. Answer the questions.

1. What was Great Barrington's problem?
2. Who organized the cleanup?
3. What were some of the things people removed?

C. Talk about your community. Has your community started any projects like the one in Great Barrington? Do you think your community needs any projects like this one?

Structure Base

A. Study the example.

Glass is	brought to the recycling center.
Cans are	

B. What happens to trash at the recycling center?
Write the correct form of the verb. Follow the examples in A.

1. Glass _____is separated_____ **(separate)** from metal.

2. Newspapers _____ **(tie)** with string.

3. Plastic bottles _____ **(flatten).**

4. All the trash _____ **(recycle).**

C. Study the example.

The window was	broken by a burglar.
The windows were	

D. Answer the questions.
Change the form of the verbs. Follow the examples in C.

1. The police _____were called_____ **(call)** by my neighbor.

2. The report _____ **(write)** by Officer Washington.

3. The damage _____ **(repair)** by the owner.

E. Study the examples.

I	like prefer love start	walking to walk	in the park at 6:00 A.M.

F. Follow the examples in E. Write about yourself.

1. I like _____.

2. I prefer _____.

3. I start _____.

4. I love _____.

G. Study the examples.

I'm	interested in tired of used to worried about thinking about	living in the city.

H. Complete the sentences. Write the –ing form of the verb.

1. I'm worried about _____staying_____ (stay) in the city.

2. I'm tired of _____ (drive) in the traffic and

   _____ (breathe) the dirty air.

3. I'm used to _____ (live) close to where I work.

4. I'm thinking about _____ (move) to the country.

5. I'm interested in _____ (rent) a house outside
   Smithville.

Write It Down

A. The community of Bayside is concerned about crime and pollution. The people want to meet to talk about what they can do. Look and read.

Bayside *Community Meeting*

Where: CITY HALL	When: MONDAY, 6 P.M.	Topic: ACTION PLAN

Please join us for a discussion of the Action Plan. Discussion will focus on these problems and solutions.

Crime

1. Hire more police to patrol the downtown area.
2. Add street lights to Pine Street.

Air Pollution from Traffic

1. Lower the cost of riding the bus.
2. Display posters to encourage the use of public transportation.

Solid Wastes

1. Form a clean-up committee.
2. Fine people who pollute.
3. Organize a day for recycling used items.

About You

B. Think about problems your community has. Plan a community meeting for people to talk about what they can do to solve these problems. Write an announcement like the one in A.

COMMUNITY MEETING TOPICS

Name of Community

Problem: _____   Problem: _____

_____   _____

What to do: _____   What to do: _____

_____   _____

I. Practice the dialog.

➤ Do you have much **crime** in **Grovemont**?

● No, we don't. Grovemont is very safe.

➤ What about **air pollution**?

● Well, that's a problem. There's lots of smog.

➤ Is water pollution a problem, too?

● Yes. The river that runs through Grovemont is polluted.

2. You want some information about Center City. Follow the dialog in I. Ask Student B about the problems. Circle the answers.

  a. air pollution   (yes)   no

  b. water pollution   yes   no

  c. noise pollution   yes   no

  d. crime   yes   no

3. Student B has some questions about Norwood. Use the picture to answer the questions.

Norwood is a noisy, crowded place. People worry about crime, but they enjoy the clean air and water.

4. Switch roles. Turn to page 54. Complete 2 and 3.

One To One

I. Practice the dialog.

➤ Do you have much **crime** in Grovemont?

● No, we don't. Grovemont is very safe.

➤ What about **air pollution**?

● Well, that's a problem. There's lots of smog.

➤ Is **water pollution** a problem, too?

● Yes. The river that runs through Grovemont is polluted.

2. Student A has some questions about Center City. Use the picture to answer the questions.

Center City is not noisy or crowded. Crime is not a problem, but the air and water are polluted.

3. You want some information about Norwood. Follow the dialog in I. Ask Student A about the problems. Circle the answers.

a. air pollution   yes   (no)

b. water pollution   yes   no

c. noise pollution   yes   no

d. crime   yes   no

4. Switch roles. Turn to page 53. Complete 2 and 3.

Extension

A. Look and read.

What Can I Do?

There are many things you can do in your own home to help clean up the environment. Here are a few tips:

Use vinegar to clean glass and mirrors.
Use vinegar and water instead of expensive window cleaner sprays. Store-bought window cleaners release tiny drops of ammonia that can be irritating to your eyes and nose. Vinegar and water makes a great, cheap, safe window and glass cleaner.

Grow spider plants.
The spider plant has always been a popular house plant because it grows fast and is almost pest-free. Even people who usually have trouble with plants can grow spider plants. Also, it has been discovered that spider plants help clean the air by absorbing harmful formaldehyde vapors.

Use cloth napkins.
Use cloth napkins instead of paper napkins. Making paper napkins uses up trees and requires a lot of energy.

Cloth napkins are washable and reusable, and they come in many pretty patterns and colors.

B. Read the questions. Write the answers. Use the article in A.

1. What can you use for cleaning windows instead of aerosol sprays? _____ vinegar _____

2. What kind of plant will help clean the air in your home? _____

3. What harmful vapors do spider plants absorb? _____

4. How can you help save trees and energy? _____

C. Work with a partner.
Talk about what you already do at home to help protect the environment. What else could you do?

Check Your Competency

Can you use the competencies?

- ☐ 1. Identify environmental problems
- ☐ 2. Identify community problems
- ☐ 3. Read about environmental solutions

**A. Use competency I. Look at the pictures.
What are the problems? Write the answers.** ✔

| noise pollution   crime   air pollution   traffic |

1. _____traffic_____   2. _____

3. _____   4. _____

B. Review competency 2. Look and read.

NEWARK, NJ

For as long as Helen Kilpatrick could remember, thieves had used the vacant lot across from her house as an open-air shop for dismantling stolen cars. The lot was a menace, not to mention an eyesore: Car bodies were scattered beside discarded mattresses, appliances, and urban debris. Kilpatrick complained to Helen Poch, president of the North District Police Community Council. She hoped Poch would raise the issue at the next council meeting, but Poch suggested a different tack: "Why don't you put in some gardens?" So Kilpatrick started the Green Horizons Community Garden.

In the summer of 1984, the junk was removed and five gardens were planted. By 1987, the number had grown to 15. In 1990, more than 40 gardeners cared for 90 separate 20-by-20 foot plots, producing $50,000 worth of vegetables a season. Green Horizons had become the largest member of Rutgers University's Urban Gardening Program. ■

Use competency 2. Read the sentences. Circle *yes* or *no*. Use the article.

1. There was a parking lot near Helen Kilpatrick's house.   yes   (no)

2. She was concerned about a lot filled with trash.   yes   no

3. The president of the community council suggested that gardens be planted in the lot.   yes   no

C. Review competency 3. Look and read.

Litter is a problem in almost every community. Litter costs you money and ruins your local environment. When you see someone littering in public, do something. Tell them you do not think that littering is acceptable. If enough people complain, it may stop people from continuing to litter.

In addition to looking bad, litter is also dangerous to wildlife. Birds can choke on plastic, and small animals can become very sick by eating litter when they are hungry. Litter also attracts rats, mice, and other pests.

Use competency 3. Answer the questions. Use the article.

1. What can cost your community money?
2. How is litter dangerous to wildlife?
3. What can you do when you see someone littering?

Food

Unit Competencies

1. Identify kinds of stores
2. Understand unit cost
3. Read ingredients on food packages

Where are the people? What are they doing? What do you think?

Read the sentences.

Van Tha Hong saves money by shopping at the farmers' market. The produce is much fresher than the supermarket produce.

Linda Santos often stops at a convenience store to buy milk. It's expensive to buy food at a convenience store, but Linda can shop there without waiting in line.

Eric Johnson loves to cook Italian, Chinese, Vietnamese, and Mexican food. He shops at ethnic food stores such as Oriental markets and Spanish grocery stores.

Lynn Hanson shops at a French bakery on special occasions. She always goes there to order birthday cakes for her children's birthdays.

Starting Out

A. Look and read.

1. Farmers bring fresh fruits and vegetables to open-air markets several times a week. The prices are usually low.

2. Many convenience stores are open 24 hours a day. You can buy drinks, snacks, and many other things.

3. Ethnic food stores sell Oriental, European, Latin American, and other kinds of foods.

4. A bakery is a good place to buy fresh bread, rolls, and pastries. You can also buy cakes and desserts for special occasions at most bakeries.

B. Answer the questions.

1. What's the difference between ethnic food stores and supermarkets?
2. Where do you usually shop for food? Why?

Talk It Over

 A. Betty is talking to her friend about shopping. Practice the dialog.

➤ **Betty,** where's the best place to buy **bread?**

● At a **bakery. Mondello's bakery** is very good.

B. Talk to your classmates. Use the dialog in A to talk about the best place to shop for each food. Write _Farmers' Market, Spanish Grocery, Oriental Market, Convenience Store, Bakery,_ or _Supermarket._

	Store
1. milk	
2. cake	
3. peaches	
4. soy sauce	
5. tortillas	
6. fresh bread	
7. apples	

 C. Work with a partner. Talk about other groceries you buy. Where do you buy them? Why do you buy them there?

Word Bank

A. Study the vocabulary.

Shopping Words		bakery
brand name	pound	convenience store
bulk	produce	farmers' market
generic	product	Oriental market
ounce	unit cost	Spanish grocery

B. Look at the pictures.
What do they show? Circle the answers.

1. (farmers' market)
   convenience store

2. brand name
   generic

3. meat
   produce

4. bulk
   packaged food

Listening

A. Look and listen.
Write the kind of store each ad talks about.

✔

| Spanish grocery   farmers' market   convenience store |
| bakery   Oriental market |
---

1. _____ convenience store _____

2. _____

3. _____

4. _____

5. _____

Listen again. Match the store and what it sells.
Write the letter on the line.

_e_ 1. Ricardo's Spanish Grocery

___ 2. Quick Mart Convenience Store

___ 3. Mondello's Bakery

___ 4. Lee's Oriental Market

___ 5. 35th Street Farmers' Market

a. fresh fruits and vegetables
b. Chinese snow peas and cabbage
c. newspapers and magazines
d. fresh rolls and bread
e. salsa and black beans

B. Wilma and Ann are talking about shopping.
What advice does Wilma give Ann? Circle _yes_ or _no._

1. Don't shop at supermarkets.   yes (no)

2. Shop only once a week.   yes   no

3. Plan your meals and make a shopping list.   yes   no

4. Shop at a convenience store whenever possible.   yes   no

5. Always buy foods that are canned and packaged.   yes   no

C. Work with a partner.
Do you agree with Wilma's advice? Why or why not?

Reading

A. Look and read.

$mart $hopper

*I*t's easy to buy products that come in pretty packages. Be careful, though. In general, the most expensive items come in the fanciest packages.

You can be a smart shopper by choosing for value, not for looks. Choose generic products. These products don't have brand names, and they usually come in the plainest packages. Generic products offer the best value and the lowest prices.

Be smart by buying the largest amount of a product. Almost always, you'll pay less if you buy items by the pound or ounce—the unit price will be lower for larger sizes than for smaller ones. And large sizes last longer, so you'll save money by shopping less.

It's wise to buy food in bulk whenever you can. That means buying foods that are unpackaged. Unpackaged items are usually cheaper. You also can buy the exact amount that you need, so there's no waste. Rice, beans, nuts, and flour are often sold in bulk.

Remember that fancy packages cost shoppers money. The next time you reach for a fancy package, stop and remind yourself, "Don't be fooled by pretty looks!"

B. Read the questions. Write the answers.

1. Which are cheaper, generic products or brand-name products?

   <u>   generic products   </u>

2. Which are usually the better buy, smaller packages

   or larger packages? _____

3. What kinds of food are often sold in bulk?

   _____

C. Work with a partner.
Talk about the kinds of products you buy.

Structure Base

A. Study the examples.

You can save money	by	buying in bulk.
	without	

B. Complete the sentences.
Add *–ing* endings to the verbs. Follow the examples in A.

1. Linh saves money by _____buying_____ **(buy)** products that are on sale.

2. He never shops without _____ **(compare)** prices.

3. He keeps costs down by _____ **(look)** for sales.

4. He never goes to the store without _____ **(make)** a shopping list first.

5. He saves money by _____ **(plan)** meals for a week.

C. Work with a partner.
Discuss ways you can save money on your food bills.

D. Study the examples.

It's	cheap	to buy in bulk.
	hard	
	convenient	

About You

E. Complete the sentences. Use your own words. Follow the sentences in D.

1. It's fun _____.

2. It's hard _____.

3. It's convenient _____.

4. It's cheap _____.

5. It's expensive _____.

6. It's boring _____.

7. It's nice _____.

8. It's easy _____.

About You

F. Work with a partner. Where is it cheap to shop? Where is it expensive to shop?

Write It Down

A. Sometimes an item costs less when you buy it in larger packages. For example, which is cheaper, five I-pound boxes of detergent or one 5-pound box of detergent? Circle the letter.

a.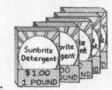

b.

B. Which product has the lower unit cost? Circle the letter.

1. (a.)

   b.

2. a.

   b.

3. a.

   b.

C. Look at the pictures. Write a shopping list for the products that have the lower unit cost. Add any other items you buy that might be less expensive if you bought them in larger quantities.

Shopping List

5-pound box of detergent

I. Practice the dialog.

➤ How much is bulk rice at Food City?

● 25¢ a pound.

 2. You want to know the prices and amounts of these products at Food City. Follow the dialog in I. Ask Student B. Write the answers.

25¢ a _____ pound _____   _____ for a _____

_____ for a _____   _____ for an _____

 3. Student B wants to know some prices at Tim's Market. Answer Student B's questions.

4. Switch roles. Turn to page 68. Complete 2 and 3.

I. Practice the dialog.

➤ How much **is bulk rice** at **Food City?**

● **25¢ a pound.**

2. Student A wants to know some prices at Food City. Answer Student A's questions.

3. You want to know the prices and amounts of these products at Tim's Market. Follow the dialog in I. Ask Student A. Write the answers.

99¢ for a __2-pound package__   _____ for a _____

_____ for a _____   _____ a _____

4. Switch roles. Turn to page 67. Complete 2 and 3.

Extension

A. Look and read.

Ingredients: Potato flakes, vegetable oil, and citric acid

Ingredients: Potato flakes, vegetable oil, sodium bisuflate, calcium stearoyl lactylate, BHA and BHT, sodium acid pyrophosphate, citric acid

Some packaged foods contain ingredients that may not be good for us. Some people believe that ingredients such as these may be harmful if we eat them frequently:

- Chemicals such as *sodium bisulfite* (to keep color), *calcium stearoyl lactylate* (to make food fluffy), and *sodium acid pyrophosphate* (to make food feel nice in your mouth)
- Chemicals that preserve food, such as *BHA* and *BHT*
- Very large amounts of salt (*sodium*)
- Very large amounts of sugar (also called *sucrose, dextrose, maltose,* or *corn syrup*)
- Artificial colors

Be sure to read the list of ingredients before you buy packaged foods. It can help you decide which items to buy and which ones not to buy.

B. Answer the questions. Circle the answers.

1. Which product has more ingredients?

   Beverly's Potatoes   (Special Spuds)

2. Which ingredient is in both products?

   sodium bisulfite   BHA   vegetable oil

3. Which product contains more chemicals?

   Beverly's Potatoes   Special Spuds

C. Work with a partner.
Talk about the ingredients of the two brands of potatoes. Which brand would you buy? Why?

Check Your Competency

Can you use the competencies?

☐ 1. Identify kinds of stores
☐ 2. Understand unit cost
☐ 3. Read ingredients on food packages

A. Use competency I. Match the products with the stores. Write the letters.

___C___ 1. the freshest produce   a. ethnic food stores

_____ 2. basic foods at all hours   b. convenience store

_____ 3. Chinese greens, soy sauce   ✔c. farmers' market

_____ 4. food from different countries   d. Oriental market

B. Use competency 2. Which products have the lower unit costs? Circle the products.

1. $2.00 $2.40

2.   40¢ Per pound $2.70

3. $1.50 $2.25

4. $2.50 $2.75

C. Use competency 3.
   Look and read. Circle the answers.

FANCY ONION SOUP MIX

INGREDIENTS: Dehydrated onions, salt, sugar, vegetable protein, wheat starch, vegetable oil, BHA, natural flavors, sodium bisulfate.

OLD-TIME ONION SOUP MIX

Ingredients: Dehydrated onions, salt, sugar, vegetable protein, wheat starch, vegetable oil, natural flavors.

1. Which product has more ingredients?

   (Fancy Onion Soup Mix)   Old-Time Onion Soup Mix

2. Which ingredients are found in both products?

   dehydrated onions   salt   sugar

   vegetable protein   wheat starch   vegetable oil

   BHA   natural flavors   sodium bisulfite

3. Which product contains more chemicals?

   Fancy Onion Soup Mix   Old-Time Onion Soup Mix

Unit Competencies

1. Identify kinds of stores
2. Read garage sale ads
3. Write garage sale ads
4. Read warranties

Where are the people? What are they doing? What do you think?

Read the story.

Eva Cruz has lived in the U.S. for about nine months. Although she has a good job, she still finds it hard to make ends meet. One day last week her friend, Helen Patterson, suggested that they shop at some new places. They went to yard sales, flea markets, thrift stores, and department stores that were having sales. There were real bargains on clothes, toys, small appliances, furniture, and other household items. Eva was delighted.

Starting Out

A. Look and read.

1. Many people have yard or garage sales on the weekends. They sell things that they no longer need.

2. You can save money by buying things that are on sale. Most discount and department stores occasionally have big sales.

3. You can find used items of all kinds at thrift stores. Whether you need clothes for your children or furniture, try shopping at a thrift store.

4. Many places have flea markets once or twice a week. People bring new and used things that they want to sell.

About You

B. Answer the questions.

1. Which places sell new merchandise? Which ones sell used merchandise?

2. What do you need to buy? Where do you want to buy it? Why?

Talk It Over

 A. Sam just moved into an apartment. Gilberto is giving him advice about where to shop. Practice the dialog.

> I need **a used kitchen table.** Where can I buy **one at a good price?**
● I'd try a **garage sale. A lot of people sell good used furniture at garage sales.**
> Thanks for the suggestion.

 B. Work with a partner. Use the dialog in A to talk about where you should shop for the items. Complete the chart.

Item	Place
a used kitchen table	garage sale
some used children's clothing	
some new bedroom furniture	
a used toaster	
a pair of new sneakers	

Word Bank

A. Study the vocabulary.

Places to Shop	Shopping Words	
department store	bargain	purchase
discount store	classified ad	sale
flea market	clearance	used
garage sale		
thrift store		
yard sale		

Useful Language
Thanks for the suggestion.

B. Look at the sale ad. Answer the questions.

WILSON'S DEPARTMENT STORE

ANNUAL FURNITURE CLEARANCE SALE

All furniture on sale
20-40% off!

Floor and Table Lamps

Dining Room Tables
30% off

Sofas and Chairs

20% off

40% off

1. Where's the sale?   Wilson's Department Store

2. What's on sale?   _____

3. How much are sofas?   _____

Listening

A. People call Claudia Ramiro on the Shopper's Hotline radio show to find out where to shop for bargains. Look and listen. Circle the answers.

1. What does Larry want to buy?

   a. work shirts and pants   b. bookshelves and lamps

2. What does Lena want to buy?

   a. picture frame   b. toaster

3. What does Dora want to buy?

   a. sheets and towels   b. skirts and blouses

4. What does Sal want to buy?

   a. furniture   b. jewelry

Listen again. What is Claudia Ramiro's advice? Write the answers.

1. Where should Larry shop?

   _____ garage sales _____

2. Where should Lena shop?

   _____

3. Where should Dora shop?

   _____

4. Where should Sal shop?

   _____

B. Work with a partner. Talk about what items you might shop for in these places.

1. a flea market
2. a department store
3. a garage sale
4. a thrift store

Reading

A. When people have garage sales, they often put classified ads in the newspaper. Look and read.

GARAGE SALES

3-FAMILY SALE
Sunday 8 A.M. to 2 P.M. Furniture, tools, ceiling fan, sewing machine (like new). Nothing over $80.
1900 Tallwood.

* BARGAINS * 4-FAMILY GARAGE SALE
Saturday from dawn to dusk. Dinette set, couch, kids' clothes, twin mattress sets, lawn mowers, lamps, small appliances. Much more! 5¢ to $75.
109 Brownlee.

GARAGE SALES

SUNDAY ONLY.
9 A.M. to 5 P.M. Housewares, desk, luggage, camera, beds, many other items. Men's, women's, children's clothing. 25¢ to $50.
3205 Oak Trail.

HUGE YARD SALE
Saturday, August 26. Complete household of furniture including televisions, stereos, tables, lamps, books. Don't miss this! 7 A.M. to 7 P.M.
7790 Kinney Avenue.

B. Read the questions. Circle the answers. Use the ads in A.

1. You're looking for a sewing machine. Where should you go?

   a. 1900 Tallwood   b. 7790 Kinney Avenue

2. You want to buy some children's clothing. You work all day on Saturdays. Where should you go?

   a. 109 Brownlee   b. 3205 Oak Trail

3. You want a used TV set. When can you shop at the sale on Kinney Avenue?

   a. 7 A.M. to 7 P.M. on Saturday   b. 8 A.M. to 2 P.M. on Sunday

4. Where can you buy something for as little as five cents?

   a. 109 Brownlee   b. 3205 Oak Trail

C. What do you need? Which sale would you go to? Why?

Structure Base

A. Study the examples.

> Who's having a sale?
> What's on sale?
> Where's the department store?
> When does the store open?
> Why do you want to go there?

B. Use words from A to complete the dialog.

➤ <u>Who's</u> going shopping with me?

● I will. _____ are you going?

➤ Reed's Department Store. They're having a sale.

● _____ on sale?

➤ Sheets and towels.

● Good. I need some new towels. _____ do you want to leave?

➤ How about 12 o'clock?

● That's fine.

C. Work with a partner. Make plans to go shopping together. Follow the dialog in B.

D. Study the examples.

> I bought the books. The books were on sale.
> I bought the books that were on sale.

> I bought the TV from my friend. My friend lives in Rosemont.
> I bought the TV from my friend who lives in Rosemont.

E. Write _that_ or _who_. Follow the examples in D.

1. Luis had a yard sale. The yard sale lasted all day.

   Luis had a yard sale _____that_____ lasted all day.

2. Luis sold a TV to his neighbor. His neighbor lives across the street.

   Luis sold a TV to his neighbor _____ lives across the street.

3. I found a table. The table was just what I wanted.

   I found a table _____ was just what I wanted.

4. Minh bought a bicycle. The bicycle was only $5.

   Minh bought a bicycle _____ was only $5.

5. I met two women. The women go to yard sales every weekend.

   I met two women _____ go to yard sales every weekend.

F. Complete the dialog. Write _who_ or _that_.

➤ Let's go to the flea market.

● Which flea market do you want to go to?

➤ The flea market _____that_____ is in Parkville.

● Good idea. I need a new desk.

➤ What's wrong with the desk _____ you have?

● It's really too small. I'm going to sell it to a man _____

   lives across the street.

➤ I'll pick you up at 8:00 on Saturday morning. OK?

● Fine. I have a friend at work _____ might be interested in

   going, too. I'll ask him tomorrow.

Write It Down

A. Look and read.

---

* BARGAINS * 4-FAMILY GARAGE SALE
Saturday from dawn to dusk. Dinette set, couch, kids' clothes, twin mattress sets, lawn mowers, lamps, small appliances. Much more! 5¢ to $75.
109 Brownlee.

3-FAMILY SALE
Sunday 8 A.M. to 2 P.M. Furniture, tools, ceiling fan, sewing machine (like new). Nothing over $80.
1900 Tallwood.

Mario and Celia Rivera live at 2905 Pearl Street. They are getting ready to move into a new house. Because it already has a stove and refrigerator, they need to sell the appliances that they bought last summer. They would also like to sell some clothing, baby furniture, and toys.

Write an ad that the Riveras can put in the newspaper. Give the date, time, and location for their sale.

*** Garage Sale ***

_____

_____

_____

_____

_____

B. Would you like to have a garage sale? Write an ad for the newspaper. Be sure to give the date, time, and location of the sale.

*** _____ ***

_____

_____

_____

_____

_____

_____

I. Practice the dialog.

> ➤ I need a new **dress shirt.**
> ● Try **Franklin's Department Store. Dress shirts** are **on sale.**
> ➤ Thanks for the suggestion.

2. You want to buy these items.
Ask Student B where you can buy them.
Follow the dialog in I. Circle the letter of the store.

1. a dress shirt

     a. Franklin's Department Store   b. Miller's Department Store

2. a pair of sneakers

     a. Endo's Shop   b. The Sportswear Store

3. a bathroom rug

     a. Miller's Department Store   b. Franklin's Department Store

3. Student B wants to buy some items. Read the ads.
Give Student B advice.

I. Practice the dialog.

> ➤ I need a new **dress shirt**.
> ● Try **Franklin's Department Store. Dress shirts** are **on sale.**
> ➤ Thanks for the suggestion.

2. Student A wants to buy some items. Read the ads. Give Student A advice.

SALE! SALE! SALE!
FRANKLIN'S DEPARTMENT STORE
Men's Dress Shirts
All prices half off!

KATZ'S SHOE STORE
Dress Shoes All sizes and styles.
20% off *SALE*

MILLER'S DEPARTMENT STORE
Bathroom rugs ✳ **All colors**
$8.99 each OUR BEST VALUE

THE *SPORTSWEAR STORE*
All Sneakers
$25.95   SAVE $5.00

The finest cotton T-shirts you can find.
All sizes. 25% off.
ENDO'S SHOP

Shop at the **EMPORIUM** for
Living room area rugs.
Variety of patterns.
Only $22.99

**3. You want to buy these items.
Ask Student A where you can buy them.
Follow the dialog in I. Circle the letter of the store.**

1. an arm chair

   (a.) Furniture by Rick   b. Marcy's Furniture

2. a table lamp

   a. Lamp City   b. Specialty Lamps

3. a man's dress jacket

   a. Simon's Suits   b. Checkerboard

Extension

A. Look and read.

A Word About Warranties

When you buy that shiny new toaster or great new TV, you probably want to rush straight home and try it out. But before you start using your new purchase, take a close look at something that comes with it—the warranty.

A *warranty*, like the one here, is a written promise by the manufacturer to replace or repair the product if it is defective in materials or workmanship. After you buy a product, check to be sure all the parts are included in the package. Do they all work? Is the quality of the merchandise satisfactory to you?

If you discover any problems, return your purchase to the store where it was purchased right away. Later, if the product breaks or stops working, send it to the address in the warranty. Most warranties give you a limited amount of time after the date of purchase in which to return a defective product. So make sure you send the merchandise back before this time limit expires.

If you damage or break the merchandise yourself, the warranty will not cover its replacement or repair. Used items are also not covered by a warranty.

ONE-YEAR LIMITED WARRANTY

Toasters, Inc. warrants this product for one year from purchase date against defects in material or workmanship. Defective products may be brought to the place of purchase, to any authorized dealer, or may be sent to Toasters, Inc., National Service Department, 2090 Pine Street, Dunesville, IN 46136 for free repair or replacement at our option. Warranty does not include: cost of inconvenience, damage due to product failure, transportation damages, misuse, abuse, accident, or the like. For more infomation, write to Vice-President of Consumer Affairs, Toasters Inc., 100 Park Avenue South, New York, NY 10010. Send name, address, ZIP Code, store or service center involved.

Answer the questions.

1. What's a warranty?
2. Why is it important to read the warranty?

B. Does the warranty in A cover these things? Circle *yes* or *no.*

1. Your new toaster breaks when you accidentally drop it on the floor.   yes   (no)

2. Your toaster no longer works after five years.   yes   no

3. You followed all of the instructions, but after a month your new toaster stops working.   yes   no

Can you use the competencies?

- ☐ 1. Identify kinds of stores
- ☐ 2. Read garage sale ads
- ☐ 3. Write garage sale ads
- ☐ 4. Read warranties

A. Use competency 1. Match the word and its definition.

__c__	1. flea market	a. a store that sells used items
_____	2. thrift store	b. a large store which sells clothing, appliances, and housewares
_____	3. department store	✔ c. an outdoor market where people bring new and used things they want to sell

B. Use competency 2. Read the ads. Circle the answers.

GARAGE SALES	GARAGE SALES
2-FAMILY SALE Lots of clothes for the whole family, large bookshelf, kids' bicycles, dishes, and baby furniture. 2906B Westhill Drive. Saturday 9 A.M. to 3 P.M., Sunday 9 A.M. to 1 P.M.	**YARD SALE**–Sunday only, March 15. Color television, dinner table, sewing machine, stereo, furniture, mattress set, futon, books, and more. 10 A.M. to 2 P.M. 6030 Jessie Street

1. You want to buy baby items for your child. You work on Saturdays. Where should you go?

    a. 6030 Jessie Street   (b.) 2906B Westhill Drive

2. Which item is being sold during the yard sale on Sunday only?

    a. sewing machine   b. tools

3. When can you shop at the sale at 2906B Westhill Drive?

    a. Saturday 9 A.M. to 3 P.M.   b. Monday 10 A.M. to 2 P.M.

C. Use competency 3. You have some old furniture and clothes that you want to sell. You want to have a garage sale. Write an ad. Give the date, time, and location of the sale.

*** Garage Sale ***

_____   _____

_____   _____

_____   _____

_____   _____

_____   _____

_____   _____

D. Review competency 4. Read the warranty.

LIMITED WARRANTY

Quality Clocks are warranted to be free of defects in material and workmanship for five years from purchase date. In the event of a defect under this warranty, we will, at our option, repair or replace the product, if you return the product postage prepaid to Quality Clocks Company, 832 Hyland Avenue, Pasadena, CA 91107, together with a check in the amount of $3.00 to cover the cost of handling. Please also include your name and address and an explanation of the defect. This warranty does not cover defects caused by misuse or improper handling.

Use competency 4. Read the sentences. Write *yes* or *no.*

1. Quality Clocks will repair or replace your clock
   if the construction or materials are defective. _yes_

2. You can use the warranty to help you have the clock
   repaired if you drop and break it. _____

3. The clock is covered by the warranty if a part falls
   off the clock four years after you buy it. _____

Home

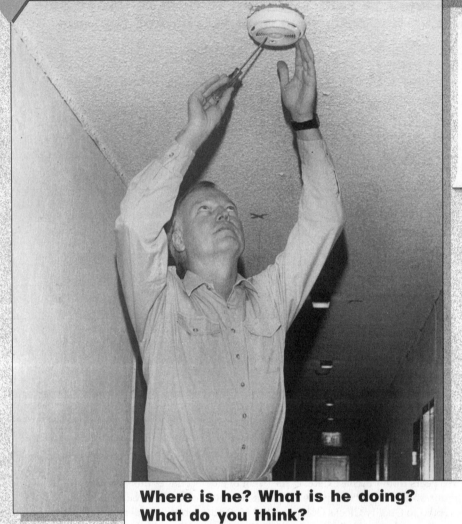

Unit Competencies

1. Correct household hazards
2. Request repairs
3. Write complaint letters
4. Read leases

Where is he? What is he doing? What do you think?

Read the story.

Pablo and Luz Rivera and their children were sound asleep in their apartment. Suddenly, the beeping of the smoke detector woke them up. When they opened their bedroom door, they could smell smoke coming from the living room.

Pablo and Luz woke their children up, and they all left the apartment. Their neighbors called 911. Two fire trucks arrived right away and put out the fire. The fire chief told the Riveras that the blaze started because there were too many plugs in a wall outlet in the living room. Because the smoke detector warned them in time, very little in their apartment got burned, and no one got hurt.

Starting Out

A. Look and read.

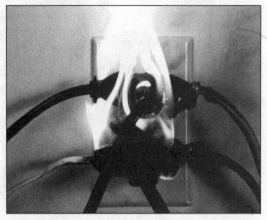

1. Windows and stairs could be dangerous places for young children. Use safety bars and gates to prevent falls.

2. This outlet has too many plugs. Putting more than two plugs into an outlet could cause a fire. Cover unused outlets with a safety cap so children won't get shocked.

3. Hanging clothes near a gas or electric heater is dangerous. Dry your clothes in a dryer, over the bathtub, or outside on a clothesline.

4. Installing a smoke detector in your home can save lives. You must check your smoke detector regularly to make sure it has fresh batteries and is working properly.

About You

B. Answer the questions.

1. How can you help keep children safe at home?
2. How can you help prevent fires in your home?

Talk It Over

 A. Mei Ling and her husband are talking in their apartment. Practice the dialog.

> ➤ I'll plug the new lamp into this outlet.
> ● Don't plug it in there. It's dangerous.
> ➤ Why?
> ● We already have the radio and the TV plugged into that outlet. A third plug could be a fire hazard.
> ➤ OK. I'll use another outlet.

About You **B. Work with a partner. Find three safety hazards in the picture. Discuss how you would fix each hazard.**

Word Bank

A. Study the vocabulary.

electrical plugs	**Safety**	install
outlet	battery	plug in
stairs	fire escape	prevent
	fire extinguisher	repair
landlord/landlady	hazards	
lease	safety bars (gates)	
tenant	safety outlet caps	
	smoke detector	

B. Look at the pictures.
Use words from A to tell what each picture shows.

1. _____ fire escape _____

2. _____

3. _____

4. _____

C. Work with a partner. Talk about things you do at home to keep yourself and your family safe.

Listening

A. These tenants want their landlord or landlady to fix something. Look and listen. Circle the answers.

1. What does Maria want fixed?

   a. a gas leak   (b.) a broken electrical outlet

2. What does Peter ask Mrs. Galvez to fix?

   a. a broken light   b. a fire extinguisher

3. What is Hector worried about?

   a. a gas leak   b. a light switch

4. What does Abby want Mr. Aquino to fix?

   a. a smoke detector   b. a broken window lock

Listen again. Who will fix the problem? Match.

1. Maria's problem   a. the maintenance man
2. Peter's problem   b. the landlord
3. Hector's problem   c. an electrician
4. Abby's problem   d. the gas company

B. Anna Ching is giving advice on a radio show. Look and listen. Circle *yes* or *no*.

1. Does Anna Ching help tenants in Roseville?   (yes)   no
2. Do tenants have to make their own electrical and plumbing repairs?   yes   no
3. Are landlords and landladies required to do certain things for tenants?   yes   no

Listen again. What does Anna Ching say landlords and landladies in Roseville must do? Circle the correct answers.

1. Put lights in hallways.

2. Buy groceries for tenants.

3. Provide emergency exits.

4. Clean the apartments every weekend.

5. Fix any plumbing or electrical problems.

6. Paint the apartments every year.

Reading

A. You just rented an apartment. There is a Tenants' Association in your town that publishes a safety check list for tenants. Complete the check list for your apartment.

ROSEVILLE TENANTS' ASSOCIATION

Your apartment must have the following safety features. This check list will help you determine how safe your apartment is. Put a check mark (✓) in front of the safety features your apartment has.

Electricity
- ❏ There are at least two outlets in every room.
- ❏ There are ceiling lights in the kitchen.
- ❏ There are ceiling lights in the bathroom.

Windows and doors
- ❏ The windows open, close, and lock securely.
- ❏ The window screens are in good condition.
- ❏ The doors unlock from the inside without a key.
- ❏ The doors open, close, and lock securely.

Heating
- ❏ The heating system is in working condition.
- ❏ The thermostats work correctly.

Smoke detector
- ❏ There is a smoke detector installed in the apartment.
- ❏ The smoke detector is in working condition.

Building
- ❏ The building hallways are well-lit.
- ❏ The building exterior is well-lit.
- ❏ The garbage area is clean and well-lit.
- ❏ The fire escape is clear and in working condition.

B. What safety features does your apartment need? Ask your landlady to fix them. Work with a partner. Follow the dialog.

➤ Mrs. Kratky, the lock on my front door is broken.

● OK. I'll fix it right away.

Structure Base

A. Study the examples.

The landlady	must	install a smoke detector in each apartment.
		repair the heating and plumbing.

The landlady	may	plant flowers outside the building.
		paint the outside of the building.

B. Complete the sentences. Circle the correct word. Follow the examples in A.

1. You **may/must** check the smoke detector regularly.

2. The apartment building **may/must** have an emergency exit.

3. The landlady told me she **may/must** paint all of the apartments this year.

4. The manager **may/must** come by today to fix the lock.

5. There is no light in the hallway. The landlord **may/must** fix it today.

6. The tenants **may/must** pay their rent every month.

C. Study the examples.

> If you touch an electrical outlet, you could get a shock.
> You could get a shock if you touch an electrical outlet.

D. Write what could happen. Follow the examples in C.

1. The light in the hallway is broken.

   <u>If the light in the hallway is broken, someone could fall down.</u>

2. Six things are plugged into one wall outlet.

   _____

3. The lock on the bedroom window is broken.

   _____

4. Clothes are drying on the heater.

   _____

E. Study the example.

> Drying clothes on a heater is unsafe.

F. Complete the sentences. Use the *-ing* form of the word.

1. <u>Installing</u> **(Install)** a safety gate at the top of stairs will prevent a child from falling.

2. _____ **(Use)** safety outlet caps will prevent children from getting shocks.

3. _____ **(Change)** a light bulb with the switch off is a safe thing to do.

4. _____ **(Check)** a smoke detector often to make sure it is working is a good idea.

Write It Down

A. Ben North asked his landlady, Ms. Storm, to install a smoke detector. It wasn't done, so Ben wrote her a letter. Look and read.

February 15, 1994

Dear Ms. Storm,

   I'm writing to remind you that my apartment does not have a smoke detector. This is a dangerous situation that has me very worried. If there is a fire, someone could get hurt. Please install a smoke detector immediately.

Sincerely,

Ben North

Ben North
Apartment 325

B. Your apartment doesn't have a good lock on the door. You've called your landlord or landlady about it several times, but nothing has been done. Write a letter.

_____
(Date)

Dear _____,

_____

_____

_____

_____

Sincerely,

_____ (Apt. _____)
(Your Name)

**I. You want to rent an apartment.
You call the landlord. Practice the dialog.**

> ➤ Does the apartment have **a smoke detector?**
> ● **Yes, there are two.**
> ➤ Does it have **two or more electrical outlets in every room?**
> ● **Yes. In the kitchen there are three.**

2. Does the apartment you want to move into have these safety features? Ask Student B. Follow the dialog in I. Mark the answers.

Feature	Yes	No
a. smoke detector	✔	
b. two or more electrical outlets in every room		
c. fire escape		
d. doors that unlock on the inside without a key		
e. hallways that are well-lit		

3. Answer Student B's questions. Follow the dialog in I. Use the floor plan.

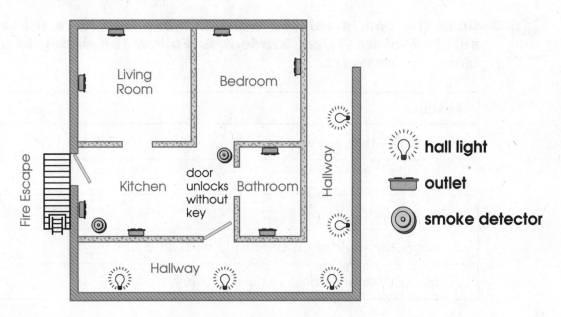

4. Switch roles. Turn to page 96. Complete 2 and 3.

**I. You want to rent an apartment.
You call the landlord. Practice the dialog.**

➤ Does the apartment have a smoke detector?

● Yes, there are two.

➤ Does it have two or more electrical outlets in every room?

● Yes. In the kitchen there are three.

**2. Answer Student A's questions. Follow the dialog in I.
Use the floor plan.**

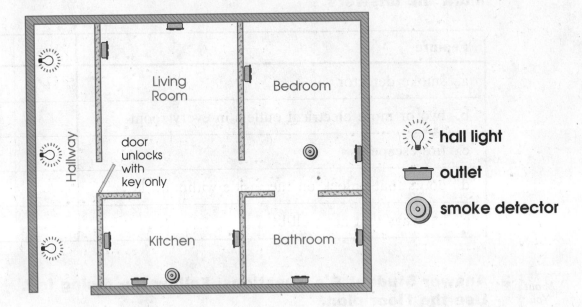

**3. Does the apartment you want to move into have these
safety features? Ask Student A. Follow the dialog in I.
Mark the answers.**

Feature	Yes	No
a. hallways that are well-lit	✔	
b. fire escape		
c. smoke detector		
d. doors that unlock on the inside without a key		
e. at least two electrical outlets in every room		

4. Switch roles. Turn to page 95. Complete 2 and 3.

Extension

A. When renting an apartment, you usually have to sign a lease. A lease is an agreement between a tenant and the owner or landlord. A lease states how long you'll rent the apartment and what you'll pay. Look and read.

❖ ════ APARTMENT LEASE ════ ❖

OWNER/LANDLORD: ___James B. Harris___   TENANT: ___Mei Ling Sung___

OWNER/LANDLORD agrees to rent TENANT an apartment in the city of ___Los Angeles___,

State of ___California___ at the following address:

Number and Street: ___304 Cypress Place___   Apartment: ___314___

Lease Term: The apartment shall be leased commencing ___May 1, 199–___,

and continue for one year until ___May 1, 199–___, at which time the lease may be renewed.

Rent: Tenant agrees to pay $ ___350___ per month, payable on the ___first___

day of each month.

Utilities: Tenant shall be responsible for the payment of gas, electricity, and water.

Deposits: The following deposits are required from Tenant prior to occupying the apartment:

One month's rent $ ___350___, security deposit $ ___250___,

TOTAL DEPOSITS DUE $ ___600___

The undersigned agree to all terms in this lease.

OWNER/LANDLORD ___James B. Harris___

TENANT ___Mei Ling Sung___

B. Read the questions. Circle the correct answers.

1. How long does the lease last?

   (a.) one year   b. two years

2. How much is the rent each month?

   a. $250   b. $350

3. Who is responsible for paying the utilities?

   a. the tenant   b. the owner/landlord

4. How much money must the tenant pay in deposits before moving in?

   a. $600   b. $250

Can you use the competencies?

☐ 1. Correct household hazards
☐ 2. Request repairs
☐ 3. Write complaint letters
☐ 4. Read leases

A. Use competency I. Which of these are household hazards? Write *safe* or *dangerous*.

1. ____safe____   2. _____   3. _____

B. Review competency 2. Complete the dialog.

✔

> problem   hallway   thanks

➤ Hello.

● Hello, **Mrs. Kratky. This is Ann Thomas in Apartment 10.** I'm calling because **the lights in the** ____hallway____ **are broken.**

➤ All right, Ann. I'll take care of the _____ today.

● _____ .

Use competency 2. The smoke detector in your apartment is broken. Use the dialog above to ask for a repair.

C. Use competency 3. You need a smoke detector in your apartment. You've asked for one many times, but you still don't have one. Your apartment manager is Ms. Pappas. Write her a letter.

```
                                    _____
                                              (Date)

        Dear _____,

        _____

        _____

        _____

        _____

                    Sincerely,

                    _____  (Apt. _____)
                         (Your Name)
```

D. Use competency 4. Look and read. Answer the questions.

```
═══════◆═══════ APARTMENT LEASE ═══════◆═══════

OWNER/LANDLORD: _____Marta Rey_____   TENANT: _____Binh Do_____

OWNER/LANDLORD agrees to rent TENANT an apartment in the city of _____Bellingham_____ ,

State of _California_ at this address: Number and Street: _703 Cypress_ Apartment: _5_

Lease Term: The apartment shall be leased commencing _April 1, 1994_ , and continue for two years.

Rent: Tenant agrees to pay $ _400_ per month, due on the _first_ day of each month.

Security Deposit: The following deposit is required from Tenant: $ _250_ .
```

1. When does the lease begin?

   a. March 18, 1994   (b.) April 1, 1994

2. On what day is the rent due each month?

   a. the first day   b. the fifth day

3. How much is the security deposit?

   a. $250   b. $400

8 Health Care

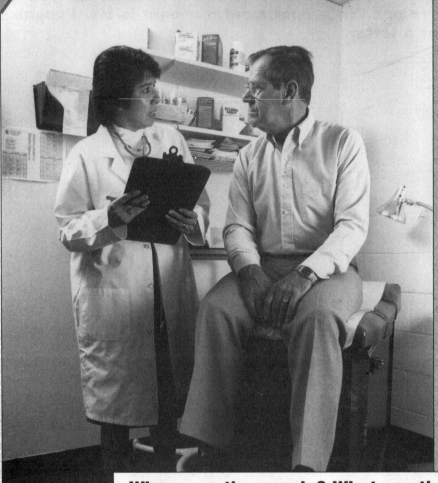

Where are the people? What are they doing? What do you think?

Practice the dialog.

> Hello, Jack. What seems to be the problem?

● I feel a little run-down, Dr. Rey. I have two jobs, so I'm tired a lot of the time.

> Two jobs! You must be busy. How much sleep do you get?

● About six or seven hours a night.

> That's not enough. You need seven or more hours every night. Are you eating OK? What is your diet like?

● Well, sometimes I don't eat lunch, or I just grab a hot dog and a can of soda.

> Jack, you need to eat three times a day. You should eat a well-balanced diet that includes a lot of fruit and vegetables.

Starting Out

1. Exercise as often as you can. Pick something that you really enjoy, such as jogging, walking, swimming, or riding your bike.

2. Eat a well-balanced diet. Remember to eat bread, fruit, vegetables, milk, and high-protein foods like chicken and beans.

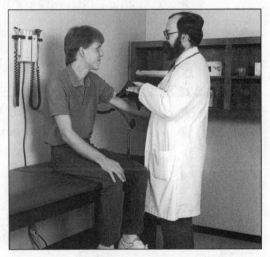

3. Get enough sleep. Most people need between seven and ten hours of sleep every night.

4. You should get a check-up every year. Your doctor can provide early treatment if there's a problem.

B. Answer the questions.

1. What kinds of food are in a well-balanced diet?
2. Why are regular check-ups important?

Talk It Over

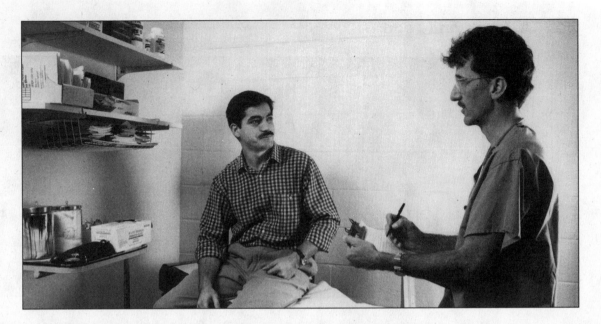

 A. Mike is a nurse. He is interviewing Abdellah before his check-up. Practice the dialog.

> How do you feel, **Abdellah?**
- **I feel great.**
> You must be taking good care of yourself. When was your last medical check-up?
- **About a year ago.**
> Do you get much exercise?
- **I think so. I ride my bike and play soccer.**
> How about your diet? What kinds of food do you eat?
- **A lot of fruit and vegetables.**
> And how much sleep do you get each night?
- **About seven hours.**

B. Talk to three students. Use the dialog in A to ask about their health habits. Write the answers.

Student	Last Check-Up	Exercise	Diet	Sleep
Abdellah	I year ago	rides bike, plays soccer	vegetables, fruit	7 hours

Word Bank

A. Study the vocabulary.

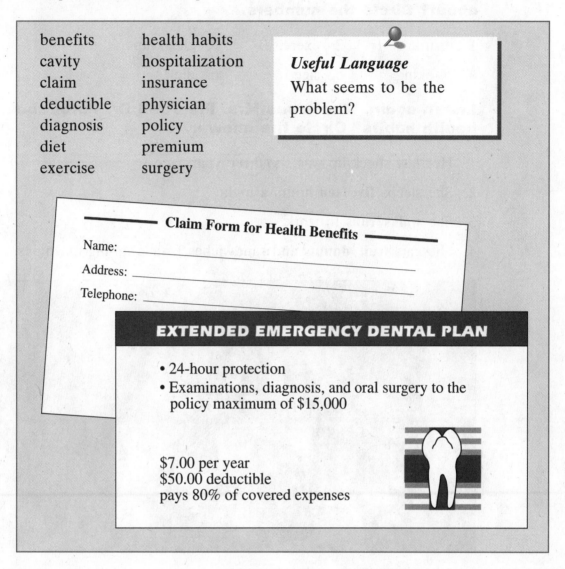

benefits
cavity
claim
deductible
diagnosis
diet
exercise

health habits
hospitalization
insurance
physician
policy
premium
surgery

Useful Language
What seems to be the problem?

Claim Form for Health Benefits

Name: _____

Address: _____

Telephone: _____

EXTENDED EMERGENCY DENTAL PLAN

- 24-hour protection
- Examinations, diagnosis, and oral surgery to the policy maximum of $15,000

$7.00 per year
$50.00 deductible
pays 80% of covered expenses

B. Use words from A to complete the sentences.

1. See a _____physician_____ once a year for a medical check-up.

2. If you need medical treatment or hospitalization, _____ can help pay the cost.

3. If you practice good health _____, you will look and feel better.

C. Work with a partner. Do you have good health habits? Have your health habits changed over the years?

Listening

A. Look and listen. What do Dr. Patel and Evelyn Field talk about? Circle the numbers.

1. insurance (2.) exercise 3. check-ups

4. smoking 5. sleep 6. diet

Listen again. What does Mrs. Field tell Dr. Patel about her health habits? Circle the answer.

1. Her last check-up was **six /(three)** years ago.

2. She sleeps **five / ten** hours a night.

3. She **walks / runs** to work.

4. She eats **fruit / donuts** and sandwiches from vending machines.

B. Benny Sakata is a famous rock star. Right now he's being interviewed on *Spotlight!* Look and listen. Circle *yes* or *no*.

1. Benny gets enough exercise.   (yes) no

2. Benny gets enough sleep.   yes no

3. Benny eats well-balanced meals.   yes no

4. Benny stopped drinking coffee.   yes no

5. Benny gets regular check-ups.   yes no

C. Work with a partner. Think about Evelyn Field's health habits. Think about Benny's health habits. Which one has better health habits? Why?

Reading

A. Look and read.

Parents can buy health insurance for their children through the public schools. There are usually several plans to choose from. Each plan gives different coverage and has a different price. The total amount you will pay is called the **insurance premium.**

STUDENT ACCIDENT INSURANCE PLANS

Select just the right coverage for your child . . . and pay a low premium.

PLAN A	PLAN B	PLAN C	PLAN D
24-HOUR PROTECTION	DENTAL	AT-SCHOOL PROTECTION	ECONOMY PROTECTION
• Before and after school • Weekends/ vacation periods • Camp and throughout summer • Effective until school starts next year	• Throughout the entire year • On and off the school premises • Examinations, diagnosis, and oral surgery to the policy maximum of $10,000	• During regular school year • On the school premises • School-sponsored activities	• During regular school year • On the school premises • Travel to and from school • School-sponsored activities
$27.00 (per year) $100.00 deductible pays 90% of covered expenses	$24.00 (per year) $100.00 deductible pays 80% of covered expenses	$22.00 (per year) $50.00 deductible pays 90% of covered expenses	$14.00 (per year) $150.00 deductible pays 80% of covered expenses

B. What does each parent want? Choose the best plan. Circle the answer.

1. Bill Moore is worried that his son might develop cavities. Which plan should he choose?

   Plan A   (Plan B)   Plan C

2. Blanca Barco wants her daughter insured at school. She wants her premium to be as low as possible. Which plan should she choose?

   Plan A   Plan C   Plan D

3. Marie Alexis needs medical insurance for her son when he is not in school. Which plan should she choose?

   Plan A   Plan C   Plan D

C. Which plan would you choose for your child or a child you know? Why?

Structure Base

A. Study the example.

> John isn't in school today. He must be sick.

B. Match. Write the letters.

__c__	1. Phil is absent from work.	a.	She must be tired.
_____	2. Oscar took the bus today.	b.	His car must be broken.
_____	3. Ming got a raise.	✔ c.	He must be sick.
_____	4. Maribel worked 12 hours today.	d.	She must be happy.

C. Write a sentence with *must be*. Follow the example in A.

1. Miguel got a new job.

   He must be happy.

2. John lost his wallet.

   _____

3. Benny runs two or three miles every day.

   _____

4. Marty never exercises.

   _____

5. The train is usually here at 10:00. It's 10:15, but the train isn't here.

   _____

6. Carolyn went to a party last night. She stayed out until 2 A.M.

   _____

7. Rupa's going to go on vacation next week.

   _____

D. Study the examples.

| She's tired. She | should
ought to
had better | get more sleep. |

She had better = She'd better

E. What should happen? Write the letters. Follow the examples in D.

___e___ 1. When she exercises, she gets tired very easily.

_____ 2. He's felt really sick for two days.

_____ 3. Without insurance, it may be difficult to pay your medical bills.

_____ 4. I haven't seen a doctor in four years.

_____ 5. We don't eat enough fruit and vegetables.

a. You'd better have a check-up soon.

b. You ought to eat a well-balanced diet.

c. He'd better see a doctor.

d. You'd better buy insurance.

✔ e. She should exercise regularly.

F. Give the people advice. Follow the examples in D.

1. I sleep four or five hours every night.

   You'd better sleep seven or eight hours a night.

2. I have a big test tomorrow.

   _____

3. I don't have time to exercise.

   _____

4. I haven't had a check-up in five years.

   _____

Write It Down

If you have an accident or illness, you must fill out an insurance claim form to receive money from your insurance company to pay for your treatment. After the insurance company checks the claim, it pays you or your doctor. Complete the form for yourself or someone you know.

CLAIM FORM FOR ACCIDENT INSURANCE

Name _____
              Last   First   Middle Name

Date of birth _____ Age _____

Address _____ City _____
       Number and Street or P.O. Box

State _____ ZIP _____ Telephone (____) ____ - _____

Date of Accident _____ 19 _____
              Month   Day

Place of Accident _____

Time of Accident _____ o'clock _____ A.M. _____ P.M.

How did the accident happen? (Describe fully.)

_____

_____

_____

_____

_____
Signature   Date

Date of Accident: _July 31, 1994_

Time of Accident: _12:30_

Place of Accident: _City Park_

What happened: _Mary was running. She fell down and broke her arm._

I. Mary had an accident. Her parents are filling out the insurance claim form. Practice the dialog.

➤ When was the accident?

● **July 31, 1994, at 12:30.**

➤ Where was the accident?

● **At City Park.**

➤ What happened?

● **Mary was running. She fell down and broke her arm.**

2. Manuel had an accident. What happened? Ask B. Complete the insurance claim form.

Date of Accident: _March 15, 1994_

Time of Accident: _____

Place of Accident: _____

What happened: _____

_____

3. Kwan had an accident. What happened? Tell B.

Date of Accident: _September 20, 1993_

Time of Accident: _7:30_

Place of Accident: _At home_

What happened: _Kwan was slicing cheese in the kitchen. He cut his hand._

Date of Accident: _July 31, 1994_

Time of Accident: _12:30_

Place of Accident: _City Park_

What happened: _Mary was running. She fell down and broke her arm._

1. Mary had an accident. Her parents are filling out the insurance claim form. Practice the dialog.

➤ When was the accident?

● July 31, 1994, at 12:30.

➤ Where was the accident?

● At City Park.

➤ What happened?

● Mary was running. She fell down and broke her arm.

2. Manuel had an accident. What happened? Tell A.

Date of Accident: _March 15, 1994_

Time of Accident: _10:45_

Place of Accident: _City Elementary School_

How the accident happened: _Manuel was playing outside. A baseball hit his face._

3. Kwan had an accident. What happened? Ask A. Complete the insurance form.

Date of Accident: _September 20, 1993_

Time of Accident: _____

Place of Accident: _____

What happened: _____

_____

Extension

A. Look and read.

Exercise and Fitness

Exercise is important to good health. Our bodies need exercise in order to be fit. There are three important kinds of fitness: muscle strength, flexibility, and heart and lung strength. Different exercises develop different kinds of fitness. Doing sit-ups or lifting weights makes your muscles stronger. Stretching exercises increase your flexibility. Running increases your heart and lung strength. Some sports, such as swimming, develop all three kinds of fitness. Also, you do not need to play a sport to get exercise. For example, if you take the stairs instead of the elevator, you will increase your heart strength. When you pick up a baby your muscles get stronger.

Lifting

Stretching

Running

B. What kind of fitness does each activity develop? Circle the letter.

1. Running five miles.

   a. muscle strength   b. flexibility   (c.) heart and lung strength

2. Lifting heavy boxes.

   a. muscle strength   b. flexibility   c. heart and lung strength

3. Playing basketball.

   a. muscle strength   b. flexibility   c. heart and lung strength

4. Moving furniture.

   a. muscle strength   b. flexibility   c. heart and lung strength

5. Doing warm-up and stretching exercises.

   a. muscle strength   b. flexibility   c. heart and lung strength

C. Work with a partner. What activities do you do? What kind of fitness does each activity develop? Do your activities develop all three kinds of fitness?

Can you use the competencies?

- ☐ 1. Identify good health habits
- ☐ 2. Answer a doctor's questions
- ☐ 3. Compare and choose insurance plans
- ☐ 4. Complete insurance claim forms

A. Use competency I. What are four ways to stay healthy? Circle the numbers.

1. Get seven or eight hours of sleep every night.

2. Eat a lot of meat at every meal.

3. Exercise as often as possible.

4. See a physician for regular check-ups.

5. Eat a well-balanced diet.

B. Use competency 2. You are having a check-up. Complete the dialog to answer the doctor's questions.

➤ When was the last time you had a check-up?

● I think _____.

➤ And how are you feeling these days?

● Well, Doctor, I feel _____.

➤ And how much exercise do you get each week?

● Oh, most weeks I _____.

➤ I see. Are you eating well-balanced meals?

● I think my diet is _____.

I eat _____.

➤ How many hours do you sleep each night?

● I usually _____.

C. Use competency 3. Choose the best plan for each parent. Circle the answer.

🏫 **PLAN C**

AT-SCHOOL PROTECTION
- During regular school year $22.00 (per year)
- On the school premises $50.00 deductible
- School-sponsored activities   pays 90% of covered expenses

🍎 **PLAN D**

ECONOMY PROTECTION
- During regular school year $14.00 (per year)
- On the school premises $150.00 deductible
- Travel to and from school   pays 80% of covered expenses
- School-sponsored activities

---

1. Jun Wong wants to pay a low yearly premium for insurance for her son.

   Plan C   (Plan D)

2. David Brodsky wants his daughter insured when she walks to and from school.

   Plan C   Plan D

3. If there is an accident, the Doyles want the insurance company to pay as much as possible of the expenses.

   Plan C   Plan D

D. Use competency 4. Your child or a child you know had an accident yesterday. Complete the insurance claim form.

Date of Accident: _____ 19 _____

Place of Accident: _____

Time of Accident: _____ o'clock _____ A.M. _____ P.M.

What happened: _____

_____

Employment

Who are the people? What are they saying? What do you think?

Practice the dialog. Mario Russo, owner of Russo's Steak House, wants to speak to Pablo Alvarado, one of the employees.

➤ Pablo, you've worked here part-time for over a year, and I think you're an excellent employee. You work hard, and you're always on time.

● Thank you, Mr. Russo. I'm glad to hear that. I really like working here.

➤ As you know, the restaurant is getting busier and busier every day. I'm promoting Trinh to headwaiter, and I'm looking for a new full-time waiter. Are you interested?

● Yes, I am. Thank you, Mr. Russo.

➤ You can start training next week. Congratulations!

Starting Out

A. Look and read.

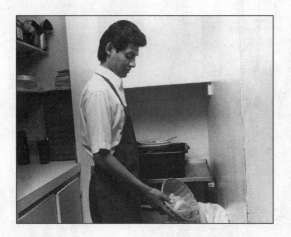

1. Working part-time clearing tables was a good beginning for Pablo Alvarado. He didn't make much money, but he worked hard and got a promotion.

2. Waiting on tables full-time is a much better job. Pablo makes more money, and he gets better benefits, too.

3. Pablo plans to start junior college soon. He wants to study food science so he can become a chef. His training will take two years.

4. Pablo's goals are to complete his studies and become a chef. He believes that hard work, determination, and education will pay off.

B. Answer the questions.

1. Why did Pablo get a promotion? Why is his new job better than his old one?

2. What are Pablo's goals? How does he plan to achieve them?

3. What are your goals? How do you plan to achieve them?

Talk It Over

 A. Practice the dialog.

➤ Pablo, are you still working at the steak house?

● I sure am. I just got a promotion. I'm a waiter now.

➤ Congratulations! How'd you do it?

● Well, my boss says I have a good attitude. Now I'm taking food science classes at City College so I can get an even better job.

➤ Really? What do you want to do?

● I'd like to be a chef.

➤ You know, that's great. I'd like to get a better job at the garage. Maybe I should take car repair classes at City College.

● That's a good idea. I have the class schedule if you want to borrow it.

B. Ask three students about jobs they'd like to have. Ask what education or training they would need. Complete the chart.

Name	Job Plans	Education or Training Needed
Pablo	chef	food science classes

Word Bank

A. Study the vocabulary.

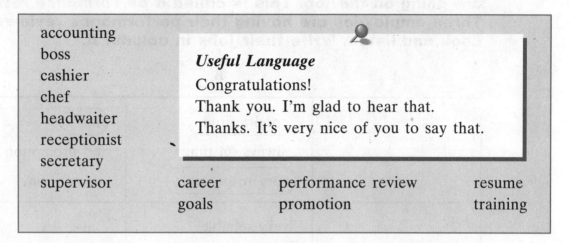

accounting
boss
cashier
chef
headwaiter
receptionist
secretary
supervisor

Useful Language
Congratulations!
Thank you. I'm glad to hear that.
Thanks. It's very nice of you to say that.

career	performance review	resume
goals	promotion	training

B. Elvira Rivera's supervisor is talking to her. Complete the dialog. Use words from A.

➤ Miss Rivera, come into my office. It's time for your

___performance review___.

● OK, Ms. Grimes.

➤ You've done excellent work this year.

● _____, Ms. Grimes.

➤ In fact, I'd like to offer you the position of assistant manager.

● Assistant manager! Thank you!

➤ You'll need to take some management _____

classes at the community college.

● Great. I've been thinking about going back to school.

➤ _____ on your _____.

About You

C. Work with a partner. Practice the dialog in B.

Listening

 A. An employer will often talk to workers about how well they are doing on the job. This is called a *performance review*. Three employees are having their performance reviews. Look and listen. Write their jobs in column A.

	A	B	C
1.	cashier	(good attitude) always on time (very responsible)	(raise) no promotion promotion
2.	_____	very reliable careful worker often late	raise no promotion promotion
3.	_____	excellent employee very reliable sometimes late	raise no promotion promotion

Listen again. What do their employers say about them? Circle the answers in column B.

Listen again. What happens? Circle the answers in column C.

 B. Katya and Ed are talking about their career goals. Look and listen. Complete the chart.

Name	Present Job	Job Plans
Katya	receptionist	
Ed		

Listen again. What kind of training will they need? Circle.

1. Katya   word processing classes   food science classes

2. Ed   English classes   accounting classes

Reading

A. In addition to paying employees' salaries, many companies offer benefits. Here are the benefits available to employees of Lake Tool Company. Look and read.

Lake Tool Company
Employee Benefits

1. Health and Medical Insurance—Employees and their families are covered by a health and medical plan partly paid for by the company.

2. Paid Sick Leave—Employees who cannot come to work because of illness will receive paid sick leave. The maximum number of sick days per year is twelve.

3. Paid Holidays—The company offers ten paid holidays each year. New Year's Day, Martin Luther King, Jr.'s Birthday, Presidents' Day, Memorial Day, Fourth of July, Labor Day, Thanksgiving and the following Friday, and Christmas Eve and Christmas Day.

4. Paid Vacation—Employees earn paid vacation after completing one year of continuous employment. See your supervisor for the number of paid vacation days you are eligible for.

5. Workers' Compensation—If you become injured on the job, insurance paid for by the company covers medical costs, a portion of your salary, and long-term disability payments, if necessary.

6. Unemployment Insurance—The company makes a yearly contribution of 1.7% of each employee's wages to unemployment insurance, so that you can draw unemployment compensation if you lose your job. The government determines the amount of money you will get and for how long.

B. Do employees at Lake Tool Company have these benefits? Circle yes or no.

1. Twelve paid holidays each year.   yes   (no)

2. Paid vacation after completing one year of work.   yes   no

3. Unemployment compensation if an employee loses his or her job.   yes   no

4. Partial salary if an employee is injured and unable to work.   yes   no

5. Medical insurance is partly paid by the company.   yes   no

C. Which benefits are important to you? Why? Which ones aren't important to you? Why?

Structure Base

A. Study the examples.

> Taking classes can help you get a promotion.
> You can start taking classes next week.

B. Elena is getting a promotion. Complete the dialog. Write the correct form of the word.

➤ Elena, I'm promoting you to manager. _____Taking_____

(take) management classes was a good idea. I think you're ready.

● Thank you very much, Tawana. When do I start working as a manager?

➤ Well, I want you to start _____ (train) sessions

right away with Virgil Haas, one of the other managers.

● Oh, good. I enjoy working with Virgil.

➤ I know what you mean. _____ (teach) managers

is one of Virgil's strong points. That's why I usually have him train

new managers. Talk to Virgil today so you can start

_____ (plan) your schedule for next week.

● OK, Tawana. Thanks again for the promotion.

➤ You're welcome. And congratulations!

About You

C. Work with a small group. Talk about what someone can do to show that he or she is a good employee. Make a list. Follow the examples in A.

Helping your coworkers shows you are a good employee.

_____

_____

D. Study the examples.

| At my current job in the hotel, I | greet | guests. |
| At my previous job in the hotel, I | greeted | |

Job description: Greeting guests.

Job description: Greeted guests.

E. Wen is applying for a job at a hotel. Complete the application. Write the correct form of the word.

H H **Hotel Hampton**
Job Application

Name: _____ Wen Chang _____

Position you are applying for: _____ hotel desk clerk _____

Present Job

Position	Job Description	
hotel desk clerk	Greeting	**(greet)** guests as they arrive.
	_____	**(help)** guests with special needs.
	_____	**(suggest)** places of interest to visit.
	_____	**(work)** with managers to complete weekly schedule.

Previous Job

Position	Job Description	
bellhop	Took	**(take)** luggage to rooms.
	_____	**(deliver)** room service orders.
	_____	**(help)** guests with special needs.
	_____	**(work)** with housekeeping to make rooms ready for guests.

Write It Down

A. Read Gloria Vega's resume. Answer the questions.

Gloria Vega

456 E. Spruce Street
Milwaukee, WI 53202
(414) 555-2145

Work Experience

Jan. 1993 - present
Secretary, Chen Brothers Import Company,
1775 Spicewood Rd., Milwaukee, WI 55301, (414) 555-4657.
Typing, filing, answering phones in English and Spanish,
translating letters and memos.

Feb. 1989 - Jan. 1993
Office Assistant, Chen Brothers Import Company.
Filed, made photocopies, and handled general office duties.

Mar. 1988 - Feb. 1989
Office Assistant, Wildwood Foods Corporation,
3237 Wisconsin St., Milwaukee, WI 55616, (414) 555-3863.
Filed, delivered company and U.S. mail to employees,
prepared packages for shipping.

Education

1988 - GED

1991 - Intensive English Program, City Learning Center.
Classes in listening, speaking, reading, and writing.

1993 - Secretarial Science Certificate, Milwaukee City College.
Courses in typing, filing, and using computers.

---

1. How many companies has Gloria worked for?
2. Where does she work now?
3. What was her first job?
4. What kind of training and education does Gloria have?

**B. Write your resume on a sheet of paper.
Follow the example in A.**

1. **An employee is asking the supervisor a question.**
   The supervisor is answering, based on the company rules.
   Practice the dialog.

   ➤ Can I buy my safety shoes through the company?

   ● Yes. You can order them from the company catalog.

2. **You're a new employee at the Shelton Furniture Company.**
   Student B is your supervisor. Ask Student B questions
   about the company rules. Follow the dialog in 1.
   Circle the answers.

   a. You want to buy your safety shoes through
      your company.   (yes)   no

   b. You want to drink coffee while you work.   yes   no

   c. You want to park in parking lot 1.   yes   no

   d. You want to take off an hour tomorrow for
      a doctor's appointment.   yes   no

3. **Student B is a new employee. You're the supervisor.**
   Use the company rules to answer Student B's questions.
   Follow the dialog in 1.

⚡ Inglewood Power Company ⚡
Company Rules

1. All employees and visitors must carry identification badges while on company property. Visitors will be issued identification badges upon arrival and must return them when they leave the premises. Lost employee identification badges must be reported to a supervisor immediately.

2. Employees must wear safety glasses at all times while on the floor. Regular glasses and sunglasses do not protect eyes from injury—they cannot be worn instead of safety glasses.

3. Employees cannot listen to radios or tape players with headphones (Walkman-type devices) while on the job. These create a hazard, since employees may not be able to hear alarms or safety warnings.

4. Employees who wish to eat lunch outside must stay in the designated picnic area on the east side of the building. Employees may not eat on the lawn in front of the building, on any of the loading docks, or in other outside work areas.

---

4. **Switch roles. Turn to page 124. Complete 2 and 3.**

One To One

Student B

1. **An employee is asking the supervisor a question. The supervisor is answering, based on the company rules. Practice the dialog.**

➤ Can I buy my safety shoes through the company?

● Yes. You can order them from the company catalog.

2. **Student A is a new employee. You're the supervisor. Use the company rules to answer Student A's questions. Follow the dialog in 1.**

Shelton Furniture Company
Company Rules

1. **Employees must wear safety shoes in the factory at all times.** Safety shoes may be purchased through the company catalog or at any shoe store that carries certified safety shoes.

2. **All food and drink must be consumed in the company cafeteria.** No food or drink is allowed at desks or on the factory floor.

3. **Employees must park in parking lots 2 or 3.** Parking lot 1 is reserved for delivery vehicles and company visitors.

4. **Employees who need to leave the building must request permission from their supervisors.** Employees will be given permission to leave during their shift for personal reasons such as doctor's appointments or family emergencies.

3. **You're a new employee at the Inglewood Power Company. Student A is your supervisor. Ask Student A questions about the company rules. Follow the dialog in 1. Circle the answers.**

a. Your children visited you at work. They want to keep their identification badges. yes (no)

b. You want to wear your regular glasses at work instead of safety glasses. yes no

c. You want to listen to your tape player with headphones while you work. yes no

d. You want to eat lunch outside in the picnic area. yes no

4. **Switch roles. Turn to page 123. Complete 2 and 3.**

Extension

A. Look and read.

Section 1　The County Times

Navajo Woman Charges Employment Discrimination

Luci Yava is a Navajo woman who claims that she is a victim of employment discrimination. The Equal Employment Opportunity Commission (EEOC) is taking her case to court. The EEOC was established by the Civil Rights Act of 1964. The Civil Rights Act prohibits discrimination based on a person's color, race, national origin, religion, or sex.

Ms. Yava worked for the Capital Corporation for five years. She says that during that time she was not given a promotion although several co-workers with less experience were promoted. None of those workers was from a minority background. Ms. Yava says she tried to discuss this issue with her supervisor, but he refused to talk with her about it.

Finally Ms. Yava contacted the United Way, a national organization with a free information and referral service. She was referred to the Human Rights Commission, which referred her case to the EEOC.

Luci Yava's case has yet to be decided. Officials at the Capital Corporation would not comment on the matter.

B. Answer the questions.

1. What kind of problem did Luci Yava have?
2. What's the first thing she did about her problem? What happened then?
3. What's the EEOC? What is the EEOC going to do for Luci Yava?
4. Do you know anyone who's been discriminated against at work? If so, in what way?

Can you use the competencies?

- ☐ 1. Talk about education, work experience, and career plans
- ☐ 2. Identify traits of good employees
- ☐ 3. Talk about rules at work
- ☐ 4. Identify job benefits

A. Review competencies I and 2. Complete the dialog.

✔

promotion   classes   time   review   hard

➤ Mr. Washington, I'm ready for my performance

review_____ .

● Fine, Temo. Come in and sit down.

➤ Thank you.

● Temo, let me start by saying you are one of our best employees.

You are always on _____ and you work _____ .

➤ Thanks, Mr. Washington.

● Are you interested in moving up from headwaiter to cook?

➤ Yes, I am.

● Well, you will need to take _____ in food science.

If you do well in your classes, we will be able to give you a

_____ .

Check Up

Use competencies I and 2. Write about your education, work experience, and career plans.

_____

_____

_____

**B. Use competency 3. Read the company rules.
Answer the questions.**

Feldon Plastic Company
Company Rules

1. Employees must park in parking lots 2 or 3. There is no employee parking in parking lot 1.

2. All food and drinks must be consumed in the cafeteria. No eating or drinking in work areas.

3. Employees must wear badges when in the building. They cannot take their identification badges home.

---

1. Can employees park in parking lot 2? _____yes_____

2. Can employees drink coffee while they're working? _____

3. Can employees take their identification badges home? _____

**C. Use competency 4. Read about the company's job benefits.
Answer the questions.**

Grassly Clothing Company
Employee Benefits

1. Health and Medical Insurance—Employees and their families are covered by a health and medical plan partly paid for by the company.

2. Paid Sick Leave—Employees who cannot come to work because of illness will receive paid sick leave. The maximum number of sick days per year is ten.

3. Paid Holidays—The company offers eight paid holidays each year: New Year's Day, Martin Luther King, Jr.'s Birthday, Fourth of July, Labor Day, Thanksgiving and the following Friday, and Christmas Eve and Christmas Day.

---

1. Does the company partly pay for medical insurance? _____yes_____

2. Do employees receive ten paid sick days per year? _____

3. Do employees get a paid holiday on Memorial Day? _____

Transportation and Travel

Where are these people? What are they saying? What do you think?

Practice the dialog.

➤ Eva, you know a lot about cars, don't you?

● Yes, a little, I guess. Why? Are you having trouble with your car, Tom?

➤ Yes, I am. I keep having problems getting the engine started. And once I get it going, it doesn't run smoothly.

● Have you taken the car in for a tune-up lately?

➤ A tune-up? That's something you do with older cars, isn't it? This car isn't even two years old.

● You should get a tune-up at least once a year no matter how new the car is. If your car is tuned up regularly, it'll run better. You should also get the oil changed about every three months.

➤ Really? Thanks for the advice. I'll take my car in for a tune-up later this week.

● Don't forget to get the oil checked, too.

Starting Out

A. Look and read.

1. A car engine needs regular care. Every three months you should check the water in the radiator and the transmission fluid, and have the oil changed.

2. If you live in a place with cold winters, make sure you've prepared your car for winter. Put in fresh antifreeze to protect your engine.

3. Always keep a spare tire and carry a car jack, a flashlight, and jumper cables in your car. You might need this emergency equipment if your car breaks down on the road.

4. Don't go over the speed limit. Prevent accidents by staying within the speed limit and following all the traffic laws.

B. Answer the questions.

1. Why is it important to take good care of a car?
2. Do you have a car? Which of these maintenance procedures and safe driving practices do you follow?

Talk It Over

 A. Practice the dialog.

> ➤ Connie, how long have you driven a car?
> ● For about five years.
> ➤ Have you ever gotten a speeding ticket?
> ● Yes, I have, but only once. I was going 40 miles per hour in a 30-mile-an-hour zone.

B. Follow the dialog. Talk to 5 or 6 other students. Ask about their driving. Write their names as they answer the questions.

_Connie_____ has driven for five years and has only gotten one traffic ticket.

_____ has never been in an accident.

_____ has never driven a car.

_____ has driven for three years and always wears a seat belt.

_____ usually obeys the speed limit.

_____ doesn't have a driver's license but wants to get one.

_____ always carries emergency equipment in his or her car.

_____ doesn't like to drive.

_____ just got a driver's license this year.

Word Bank

A. Study the vocabulary.

Maintenance and Repair Words		Car Safety	
	oil	**Car Safety**	spare tire
Repair Words	overheating	flashlight	speed limit
antifreeze	radiator	jack	traffic ticket
battery	recharge	jumper cables	
brake fluid	transmission fluid	mechanic	
brakes	tune-up	seat belt	

B. Read the car safety checklist. Complete the sentences. Use the words from A. Check off the things you have done.

Car Maintenance and Safety Checklist

Owning and driving a car is a big responsibility. To be safe and to save money, be sure to follow these suggestions:

❑ Put in _____antifreeze_____ in the winter.

❑ Check the _____ fluid every three months.

❑ Change the _____ every three months.

❑ Always wear a _____ .

❑ You should keep a _____ in your car in case you have a flat tire.

C. Read the sentences. Are they taking good care of their cars? Are they driving safely? Circle *yes* or *no*.

1. Eric hasn't changed the oil in his car since last year.   yes (no)

2. Tina always wears her seat belt.   yes no

3. Ming puts new antifreeze in her car every November.   yes no

4. Al had a flat tire, but he didn't have a jack in his car.   yes no

5. Millie got three speeding tickets last year.   yes no

Listening

 **A. Look and listen. What's the problem with their cars?
Circle the answer.**

1. Doris Morita   (a.) The car oil light   b. The headlights don't
                        keeps coming on.   work.

2. Ben Jones   a. There's a smell of   b. The car won't always
                        gas.   start.

3. Mrs. Solera   a. There are noises and   b. There's smoke coming
                        a smell of something   from the engine.
                        burning.

Listen again. What advice does each mechanic give?

1. <u>Bring the car in to check for an oil leak.</u>

2. _____

3. _____

 **B. Rita just bought a car. What does the salesman say she
should do to take care of her car? Circle the answers.**

(1.) Have the oil changed every three months.

2. Have a tune-up every year.

3. Wash the car every week.

4. Check the water in the radiator regularly.

 **C. Have you or someone you know ever had any car trouble?
Talk about what happened.**

Reading

A. Look and read.

HIGH/LOW ANTIFREEZE & COOLANT
Keep your engine temperature steady.
Use High/Low in your engine's cooling system.

High/Low gives your car's cooling system all the protection it needs against rust and corrosion. For best protection, replace High/Low once a year.

FIGHT WINTER FREEZE-UPS WITH High/Low.
- For most cars, a 50/50 mix of High/Low and water is all the protection needed. Protects against temperatures down to −34°F.
- If it gets really cold, use a 70/30 mix of High/Low and water. Protects down to −84°F.

FIGHT SUMMER BOILOVERS WITH High/Low.
- For most cars, use a 50/50 mix of High/Low and water. This raises the boiling temperature of your cooling system to 265°F.*
- If it gets really hot, use a 70/30 mix of High/Low and water. This raises the boiling point of your cooling system to 276°F.*

* for car radiators with a 15 lb. pressure cap in good condition

B. Read the questions. Write *yes* or *no*.

1. Is High/Low Antifreeze and Coolant used to keep the engine temperature steady? _____yes_____
2. Should you replace High/Low in your car twice a year? _____
3. For very hot weather, should you use a 50/50 mix of High/Low and water? _____
4. For temperatures down to -34°F, should you use a 50/50 mix of High/Low and water? _____

C. How would you use High/Low Antifreeze and Coolant where you live? Why?

Structure Base

A. Study the examples.

I've	driven	since 1989.
He's		
She's		
We've		
You've		
They've		

B. Complete the sentences. Follow the examples in A.

1. She has a driver's license.

   She's had _____ (**have**) a driver's license for five years.

2. We own a car.

   We _____ (**own**) a car since 1988.

3. I drive a car.

   I _____ (**drive**) a car for two years.

4. They take their car to Wong's Garage.

   They _____ (**take**) their car to Wong's Garage since 1990.

5. You have a problem with your car.

   You _____ (**have**) a problem with your car since Thursday.

About You **C. What have you done since you came to the U.S.? Write three things you've done since you arrived here.**

_____

_____

D. Study the example.

> I've never changed the oil in my car.

E. Write five things you've never done. Follow the example in D.

1. _____

2. _____

3. _____

4. _____

5. _____

F. Study the examples.

> Have you ever been to New York?

Yes,	I	have.
No,		haven't.

G. Answers the questions. Follow the examples in F.

1. Have you ever owned a car?

   _____

2. Have you ever had a driver's license?

   _____

3. Have you ever driven to California?

   _____

4. Have you ever changed a flat tire?

   _____

H. Work with a partner. Talk about things you have and haven't done.

Write It Down

A. Look and read.

YOU CAN AVOID "Car Repair Blues"

You are looking under the hood of your car, trying to figure out what the mechanic is telling you. He says your master cylinder must be replaced. You are not sure why. You don't know if the price he says you have to pay is reasonable. What should you do?

Unfortunately, most automobile owners are all too familiar with this scene. In fact, auto repair is a major consumer problem. How can consumers avoid overpriced or faulty repair work?

KNOW WHAT YOU'RE PAYING FOR

➤ The repair shop should give you a written estimate for the total price of parts and labor for the specific repair work. A repair shop cannot charge you more than the estimated price or for additional work without your consent.

➤ All repair work, parts, and labor should be listed on the final invoice. If the final charge is more than the estimate you approved, you do not have to pay the amount over the original estimate.

ASK QUESTIONS

➤ Ask for advice from friends who have been satisfied with the repairs done by a particular shop.

➤ Find out how long the shop has been in business.

➤ Get a second opinion on what is wrong with your car.

➤ Find out if the shop gives written warranties. A good repair shop guarantees its work.

➤ Be suspicious of low price quotes and coupons. Find out specifically what the price does and does not include.

Do you have a complaint that was not resolved? Your local Better Business Bureau office has a customer complaint form.

B. What should they do? Write *yes* or *no*. Use the article.

1. Ben's mechanic told Ben that he needs a new engine. It'll cost a lot of money. Ben isn't sure the problem is that serious. Should he get a second opinion?   _____yes_____

2. Dennis got an estimate for having his brakes fixed. When he got the bill, it was $200 over the estimate. No one had called to tell him about the extra amount. Should he pay the extra $200?   _____

3. Linh had the oil in her car changed at a garage. The engine's had an oil leak ever since. The mechanic who changed the oil says everything is fine. Should Linh file a complaint?   _____

One To One

I. Practice the dialog.

> ➤ I'm having car trouble. Can you help me?
> ● Sure. What's the problem?
> ➤ Well, **my car doesn't always start right away.**
> ● **You should check the battery.**

2. You are having car trouble. Ask Student B what you should do. Follow the dialog in I. Write the answers.

a. Your car doesn't start right away.

    Check the battery.

b. The car doesn't run smoothly.

c. You hear a loud noise when your car stops.

3. You know a lot about cars. Student B has car trouble. Give your partner advice. Follow the dialog in I.

PROBLEM	ADVICE
The lights seem to be dim.	Check the battery.
The car's overheating.	Check to see if there's water in the radiator.
The oil light keeps coming on.	Check the engine to see if there's an oil leak.

4. Switch roles. Turn to page I38. Complete 2 and 3.

5. Ask your partner for advice about a car problem you have had. Write down your partner's advice.

I. Practice the dialog.

> ➤ I'm having car trouble. Can you help me?
> ● Sure. What's the problem?
> ➤ Well, **my car doesn't always start right away.**
> ● **You should check the battery.**

2. You know a lot about cars. Student A has car trouble. Give your partner advice. Follow the dialog in I.

PROBLEM	ADVICE
The car doesn't run smoothly.	Get a tune-up.
The car makes a loud noise when it stops.	Check the brakes.
The car won't start right away.	Check the battery.

3. You are having car trouble. Ask Student A what you should do. Follow the dialog in I. Write the answers.

a. Your car's overheating.

   <u>Check to see if there's water in the radiator.</u>

b. The lights are dim.

   _____

c. The oil light keeps coming on.

   _____

4. Switch roles. Turn to page 137. Complete 2 and 3.

5. Ask your partner for advice about a car problem you have had. Write down your partner's advice.

_____

_____

Extension

A. **If you believe that a mechanic has not repaired your car properly, you can file a customer complaint form with the Better Business Bureau. Look and read.**

CUSTOMER COMPLAINT
IMPORTANT! COMPLETE ALL 4 SECTONS - WRITE FIRMLY

1	DATE PROBLEM OCCURRED	NAME OF PERSON OR COMPANY YOU COMPLAINED TO	PRODUCT OR SERVICE INVOLVED

2 COMPANY NAME AND ADDRESS   CUSTOMER NAME AND ADDRESS

_____   _____

_____   _____

_____   _____

3 WHAT IS YOUR COMPLAINT?
(Also be sure to enclose photocopies of contracts, receipts, cancelled checks, or other relevant documents):

_____

_____

_____

_____

_____

_____

4 WHAT SETTLEMENT WOULD YOU CONSIDER FAIR?

_____

_____

	Your Signature	Date

B. **On March 3, 1993, you took your car to Honest Al's Repair Shop on 6050 Geneva Street. You signed an estimate to have an oil leak fixed. Al did the work. You brought the car back because it was still leaking. Al said the car was fine. You called again today because it's still leaking. Al won't fix it. Complete the customer complaint form in A.**

Can you use the competencies?

☐ 1. Understand car maintenance and repair

☐ 2. Identify safe driving practices

☐ 3. Complete customer complaint forms

☐ 4. Read auto product labels

A. Use competencies I and 2. Circle *yes* or *no*.

1. Having your car tuned up every year will keep it running smoothly.   (yes)   no

2. Wearing a seat belt won't protect you from injury in an accident.   yes   no

3. You should always keep a jack and a spare tire in your car.   yes   no

4. Before you have repairs done on your car, you should get an estimate.   yes   no

B. Use competency 3. Your car is overheating. You take it to Joe Forte at the E-Z Garage. He charges you $200 for the work. You call Joe a few days later to tell him the car is still overheating. You want to bring the car in. Joe says *no*. You want your money back. Complete the customer complaint form.

3	**WHAT IS YOUR COMPLAINT?** *(Also be sure to enclose photocopies of contracts, receipts, cancelled checks, or other relevant documents):*

_____

_____

_____

4	**WHAT SETTLEMENT WOULD YOU CONSIDER FAIR?**

_____

_____

	Your Signature	Date

C. Use competency 4. Look and read. Write *yes* or *no*.

UMBRELLA ANTIFREEZE AND SUMMER COOLANT
 • Year-round rust and corrosion protection.
 • Protects all metals in all cooling systems, including aluminum.

USES

• **AS A SUMMER COOLANT**

Use a 50/50 mix of Umbrella and water for protection up to +265°F.*

For extra protection, use a 70/30 mix of Umbrella and water (boiling point of +276°F*).

• **AS A WINTER ANTIFREEZE**

Use a 50/50 mix of Umbrella and water for protection down to -34°F. For extra protection, use a 70/30 mix of Umbrella and water (freezing point of -84°F).

ONCE A YEAR: Remember to flush out old antifreeze/coolant and put in fresh Umbrella Antifreeze and Summer Coolant.

*using a 15 lb. pressure cap

---

1. Can you use Umbrella Antifreeze and Summer Coolant to keep the engine cool in summer?   <u>   yes   </u>

2. Should you use a mix of 70/30 of Umbrella and water for temperatures down to -34°F?   <u>   </u>

3. Does a 50/50 mix of Umbrella and water protect the engine in temperatures up to +265°F?   <u>   </u>

Listening Transcript

Unit 1

Listening (Page 6)
Exercise A.
Look and listen. Who did Bob talk to? Circle the letter of the correct picture.

1. *[telephone ring]*
   Mom: Hello, Bob, it's Mom. How are you?
   Bob: Oh, hi, Mom. I'm OK, how are you?
   Mom: I'm fine, thanks. I haven't seen you for a while. Would you like to come over for lunch on Saturday?
   Bob: Sure. What time?
   Mom: How about 12:30?
   Bob: Lunch sounds great. I'll be there.
   Mom: See you then. Bye.
   Bob: Bye, Mom.

2. *[telephone ring]*
   Teresa: Hello.
   Bob: Hi, Teresa. It's Bob from accounting class.
   Teresa: Oh, Bob. How are you?
   Bob: Pretty good. I'm really enjoying the spring weather, and I was wondering if you'd like to go to the baseball game Friday night.
   Teresa: I'd love to, but I can't. I've already made plans for dinner with Sharon. Can we go some other time? .
   Bob: Sure. I'll call back soon.
   Teresa: Great. Thanks for calling. Enjoy the game. Good bye.
   Bob: Bye.

3. *[telephone ring, answering machine tone]*
   Ms. Lee: Hello, Bob. This is Ms. Lee, your supervisor. I'm having some people from the company over for a picnic on Saturday. I sure hope you can join us. We'll start eating around two o'clock. Give me a call to let me know if you can make it to the picnic. I'm at 555-6231.

Exercise B.
Listen again. What's the relationship of each person to Bob? Write the answer in column A. *[Play the tape or read the transcript of Exercise A aloud again.]*

Listen again. Write what the invitation is for in column B. *[Play the tape or read the transcript of Exercise A aloud again.]*

Listen again. Did the person accept the invitation? Circle the answer in column C. *[Play the tape or read the transcript of Exercise A aloud again.]*

Unit 2

Listening (Page 20)
Exercise A.
Look and listen. What are they doing? Circle the answers in Column A.

1. A: Well, you're buying a lot of vegetables today.
   B: We're having people over for dinner tonight.
   A: That'll be $42.55. Cash or check?
   B: $42.55? I think I have enough cash.
   A: Great. Here's your receipt.
   B: Thanks. See you next week.

2. A: Hi, Hana. Where are you going?
   B: To the mailbox. I'm mailing my rent check.
   A: My rent was just raised.
   B: I've been lucky. Mine is still $550.
   A: $550? That's not bad.
   B: Do you want to go with me to mail my check?

3. A: We didn't get much mail today. Just the gas bill.
   B: How much is it?
   A: It's $65.
   B: $65? Wow. It was a lot less last month.
   A: Well, it was cold this month, and we had to use the heater a lot.
   B: That's true. Do you want me to write a check for it right now?
   A: No, I've already written the check. We can mail it tomorrow.

Listen again. How did they pay? Circle the answers in Column B. *[Play the tape or read the transcript of Exercise A aloud again.]*

Exercise B.
Look and listen. Answer the questions.
Write *yes* or *no*. *[Read like a radio ad.]*
There's one bank for all your banking needs—City Bank and Trust. City Bank and Trust now offers a new Super Service Account for all your checking and savings needs. With the Super Service Account, you receive customer service 24 hours a day. You also get a variety of features—most are free and others require only a low, low charge. Here are some of the features of the Super Service Account:

♦ You pay just $5.00 for the monthly service charge. Or you pay no monthly charge at all if you keep a minimum balance of $200 in your combined checking and savings.

♦ You get unlimited check writing with no per-check charge.

♦ You get automatic payment of your car loan at no charge.

♦ You are entitled to three money orders a month at no charge.

♦ And you can make unlimited ATM deposits and withdrawals at no charge.

Those are just a few of the benefits you receive when you open a Super Service Account. To find out more, stop by City Bank and Trust. A friendly representative will be glad to tell you all the features of a Super Service Account. For easy and convenient banking, you can trust City Bank and Trust.

Look and listen again. What are the bank charges? Write the amounts. *[Play the tape or read the transcript of Exercise B aloud again.]*

Unit 3

Listening (Page 34)
Exercise A.
Look and listen. When did they come here? Show the order. Write the numbers from 1 to 5.
People from all over the world have come to the U.S. to live for many different reasons. The first group of people to arrive here was probably from Asia. These ancestors of today's Native Americans came thousands of years ago to find better hunting grounds and farmland. Some Native Americans lived in villages and farmed. Others traveled all over the new land looking for food.

In the 1500s, Spaniards came to the continent looking for adventure, wealth, and land. The Spaniards explored and settled much of what are now the southeastern and western parts of the U.S. The Spanish built cities and founded several missions on the lands they discovered.

English settlers called Pilgrims arrived in the 1600s. The Pilgrims could not practice their own religion in England, so they came to this new land for religious freedom. The Pilgrims settled in the northeastern part of the continent.

Some newcomers did not come to the U.S. by choice. Africans were forced to come to the Americas as slaves. Africans began arriving during the 1600s. In the mid-1800s slavery ended, but Africans continue to come to the U.S., though in smaller numbers.

Millions of immigrants arrived during the 1800s. Many people from China came to the U.S. at this time. Many Chinese immigrants worked building the railroads that brought more settlers to the western U.S. Many people from Ireland and Germany came to the U.S. during this period, also. They came to escape poverty and hunger. In the U.S. they could find good farmland and lots of jobs. The Irish and German immigrants also found political freedom in the U.S.

Today immigrants continue to arrive in the U.S. from all over the world. People from Southeast Asia come to the U.S. to escape wars in their own countries. Many people from Central and South America come to the U.S. looking for economic opportunities or to find political freedom. Whatever the reasons for coming here, immigrants have helped the U.S. become the unique country that it is today.

Listen again. Why did they come here? Write *yes* or *no*. *[Play the tape or read the transcript of Exercise A aloud again.]*

Exercise B.
Listen to the interview between Karma and a newspaper reporter. Karma recently immigrated to the U.S. Circle the letter of the correct answer.

Reporter: Tell me, Karma, how long have you been in the U.S.?

Karma: I arrived here in Minneapolis about three weeks ago. I was happy to get here. It was a very long trip.

Reporter: Where did you come from?

Karma: I came from Tibet, which is in Central Asia.

Reporter: That certainly is a long way. Do you still have family there?

Karma: Yes. My brother and mother are still in Tibet. I also have another brother who lives in northern India.

Reporter: What made you decide to immigrate to the U.S.?

Karma: Well, there were many reasons, but the most important was political freedom. Right now in Tibet, Tibetans don't have much political freedom. We cannot always say what we think, or do what we want.

Reporter: Thanks, Karma. I hope things go well for you in the U.S.

Unit 4

Listening (Page 48)
Exercise A.
A community action group is having a meeting to talk about some of the problems in Northridge. Look and listen. Write the solution to each problem.

Chairman: Will the meeting come to order, please? Today we're going to talk about the progress we've made solving some of the problems in Northridge. Mr. Robles will begin by discussing the crime problem.

Mr. Robles: Well, as you all know, crime is a big problem downtown. We've suggested that the city add street lights and put more police in that area after dark. I'm pleased to report that money for our requests has been funded by the city council. The street lights will be put up next month and the new police patrols have already started.

Chairman: Thank you, Mr. Robles, that's great news. Now, Mrs. Scott, will you update us on the trash problem in our parks?

Mrs. Scott: Yes, thank you. At our last meeting, I reported that we had signed up only three volunteers to pick up trash in the parks on the weekends. Since that time, however, eleven new people have offered to help. Next weekend all of the volunteers will be picking up trash in Lincoln Park.

Chairman: Wonderful. Dr. Jackson, are we making as much progress dealing with the smog problem?

Dr. Jackson: Well, we've posted signs around town, encouraging people to car-pool or to take the bus, but so far we haven't had much success getting people to change their driving habits.

Chairman: Thank you, Dr. Jackson. I suggest that we make the smog problem our main topic of discussion at our next meeting. Now, Mrs. Wong, will you update us on the noise problem?

Mrs. Wong: I'd be happy to. As you know, the biggest noise problem we have is the airport. We have written letters to the airport manager. We have asked them not to allow jets to land or take off between 11 p.m. and 6 a.m. They have agreed. Starting next month, jets will not be able to take off or land during these hours.

Chairman: Thanks, everyone, for your hard work and input. And now on to new business...

Listen again. Which problem has not been solved? Circle the answer. *[Play the tape or read the transcript of Exercise A aloud again.]*

Exercise B.
Some friends are talking about problems in the city. What's the problem? Write the answer in Column A.

1. A: Hi, Aki. What's wrong?
   B: I'm really upset.
   A: What happened?
   B: My car was broken into!
   A: Oh no! That's terrible. What was stolen?
   B: My tape deck.
   A: Maybe you should get a car alarm. They're not too expensive. That'll help prevent another robbery.
   B: Great idea! I'll try it. Where can I get one?

2. A: Don, you look great! The last time I saw you, you looked tired.
   B: I was. Some construction workers were tearing up the street where I live. They started their jackhammers around 5:00 in the morning. I wasn't getting enough sleep.
   A: What did you do?
   B: I wrote to the city council and complained about the noise.
   A: I guess it helped.
   B: It did. A city council member called me. Did you know that there's a law against making loud noises before 6:30 in the morning? When I found out, I talked to the workers.
   A: And they started work later?
   B: Yes. Now they wait until 6:30.

3. A: Just look at the smog! I've never seen the sky look so bad!
   B: I've never felt so bad. I have asthma. When it's this smoggy, I can hardly breathe.
   A: Have you talked to your doctor?
   B: Yes, I had an appointment this morning. She told me not to go outside on really smoggy days like this unless it's absolutely necessary.
   A: You'd better go straight home after work.
   B: I plan to. When the smog's this bad, I'll just travel between work and home.

Listen again. Circle what can be done in column B. *[Play the tape or read the transcript of Exercise B aloud again.]*

Unit 5

Listening (Page 62)
Exercise A.
Look and listen. Write the kind of store each ad talks about. *[Read like radio ads.]*

1. Welcome to Quick Mart! We're open 24 hours a day for your convenience. Drop by any time to pick up a gallon of milk or some bread. We've got a great selection of newspapers, magazines, and cold drinks, too. Shop without waiting in long lines. We have ten stores in the city, so we're always nearby. Come to Quick Mart— the finest convenience store in town!

2. For the freshest fruits and vegetables, come to the 35th Street Farmers' Market. We're open every Wednesday from 6 A.M. to 6 P.M. Enjoy this season's fresh celery and lettuce right off the farm. Come to the Farmers' Market for unbeatable prices and freshness.

3. Come to Ricardo's Spanish Grocery! Find the best values on salsas, black beans, rice, and all the ingredients you need for your favorite dishes. Shop at Ricardo's Spanish Grocery daily from 8 A.M. to 9 P.M.

4. For fresh bread and rolls baked daily, come to Mondello's Bakery on Charter Street. We also make cakes for all occasions. For your next birthday or anniversary party, why not come in and order one of our famous chocolate cakes? We're open from Monday through Saturday from 9 A.M. to 7 P.M.

5. Can't find the right kind of rice, soy sauce, or spice? What about fresh Chinese snow peas or cabbage? Lee's Oriental Market has the special spices and the exotic vegetables you need. Don't pass us by. Find all you need at Lee's Oriental Market. Stop in between 9 A.M. and 6 P.M. daily. You'll be glad you did!

Listen again. Match the store and what it sells. Write the letter on the line. *[Play the tape or read the transcript of Exercise A aloud again.]*

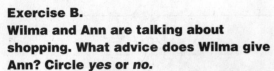

Exercise B.
Wilma and Ann are talking about shopping. What advice does Wilma give Ann? Circle *yes* or *no*.

Wilma: Welcome to the Wise Consumer Talk Show. This is Wilma Raposa. What are your shopping habits? Do you spend too much money? Does the food you buy spoil too quickly? Where can you get the best bargains and still shop wisely? Give me a call. Let's talk. Great, here's a caller now.

Ann: Hi, Wilma. This is Ann. I need help! It's hard for me to shop without spending a lot of money. Do you have any suggestions for how I can cut down on my grocery bills?

Wilma: Where do you shop?

Ann: At convenience stores, sometimes. I run into a convenience store if I'm in a hurry.

Wilma: Convenience stores are too expensive. I bet you're also shopping two or three times a week, aren't you?

Ann: Yes, I am.

Wilma: OK. Try this: Plan your meals for one week. Then make a shopping list. And shop just once a week at a supermarket, *not* a convenience store.

Ann: Let's see. Plan my meals for a week, then make a shopping list. Shop only once a week at the supermarket.

Wilma: Yes. And don't buy canned or packaged foods if you can buy them fresh. Remember, Ann, fresh is cheaper.

Ann: OK. I like fresh foods. I'll try the farmers' market on Main Street Tuesday mornings. Thanks for all your shopping tips!

Unit 6

Listening (Page 76)
Exercise A.
People call Claudia Ramiro on the Shopper's Hotline radio show to find out where to shop for bargains. Look and listen. Circle the answers.

1. Claudia: Welcome to Shopper's Hotline! This is Claudia Ramiro with tips on bargain hunting. Here's our first caller. Hello, Larry.

Larry: Hi, Claudia. I just moved into my first apartment. I have to buy a lot of things, but I'm trying hard to budget my money. Any suggestions?

Claudia: Well, the first thing you should do is shop for one room at a time. Make a list of things that you absolutely must have for that room. For example, what do you need for your living room?

Larry: I'd like some bookshelves and lamps.

Claudia: OK. Have you thought about buying used bookshelves and lamps?

Larry: No, not really. Where should I look for used furniture?

Claudia: Well, try going to garage sales.

Larry: Garage sales? Where can I find out about them?

Claudia: Look in the want ads in your newspaper. Look under "Garage Sale" or "Yard Sale."

Larry: That's a great suggestion! Thanks, Claudia!

2. Claudia: Our second caller is Lena. Hello, Lena. You're on the air.

Lena: Hi, Claudia. I want to buy a wedding gift for my friend. She's getting married in the spring. I was thinking about a nice picture frame, but I can only afford one under twenty dollars.

Claudia: A picture frame? That'll be a nice gift. For a new frame under twenty dollars, I'd try a department store.

Lena: Aren't items there expensive?

Claudia: Not always. Some department stores have great sales in spring and fall. Watch for newspaper ads for Walton's Department Store. Sometimes they advertise on television, too.

Lena: Thanks for the idea, Claudia! Good-bye.

3. Dora: Hello. I'm Dora. I'm a college student, and I need some inexpensive clothes. I've tried department store sales, but those prices are too high for me. What should I do?

Claudia: What kind of clothes do you need?

Dora: Some skirts and blouses.

Claudia: Well, how about trying a used clothing store?

Dora:	That's a good idea.		Maria Ramirez:	It's broken, and wires are hanging out.
Claudia:	Try Tony's Thrift Shop. They have a lot of used clothing that might be just right for you.		Mr. Harris:	I'm pretty busy right now, but I'll take care of it next week some time.
Dora.	I know where that is, but it's too far from my house. Do you know of any places closer to Third Street?		Maria Ramirez:	Mr. Harris, I'd like to have it fixed right away, please. I have little kids. They could get hurt.
Claudia:	Look in the yellow pages of the telephone book under "Thrift Shops."		Mr. Harris:	OK, you're right, we don't want that. I'll call an electrician right away. I'll ask him to go by and fix the outlet.
Dora:	OK, I will. Thanks a lot.			

4. Claudia: We're just about out of time. Let's take one more caller.

Sal: Hi, this is Sal. I want to find a birthday present for my wife. She loves jewelry, but I can't spend very much. Do you have any suggestions?

Claudia: I sure do! I'll tell you about one of my favorite places to go—the flea market on Skyline Road. You can find all kinds of old and new things there—from antique furniture to hand-made jewelry.

Sal: Terrific! Maybe I'll find her a necklace or earrings there. Thanks a lot!

Claudia: You're welcome. Well, that's it for today. Happy bargain hunting.

Listen again. What is Claudia Ramiro's advice? Write the answers. [Play the tape or read the transcript of Exercise A aloud again.]

Unit 7

Listening (Page 90)
Exercise A.
These tenants want their landlord or landlady to fix something. Look and listen. Circle the answers.

1. Mr. Harris: Hello? This is James Harris.s.

Maria Ramirez: Mr. Harris, this is Maria Ramirez in Apartment 204. I'm sorry to bother you, but there's an electrical outlet in my living room that needs to be fixed.

Mr. Harris: What's wrong with it, Mrs. Ramirez?

Maria Ramirez: When do you think the electrician will be here?

Mr. Harris: Probably tomorrow.

Maria Ramirez: Thank you, Mr. Harris.

2. Mrs. Galvez: Hello, Peter. How are you??

Peter: Fine, Mrs. Galvez. Thank you. I came by because the light outside our door isn't working.

Mrs. Galvez: Oh, it probably just needs a new light bulb.

Peter: No, it's not that. We changed the light bulb ourselves, and it still doesn't work. We don't feel safe without an outside light. Could you send the maintenance man out this afternoon to fix it?

Mrs. Galvez: The maintenance man won't be here until tomorrow morning, Peter. I'll send him to your apartment first thing. You're in number 19, right?

Peter: Yes, number 19. Thank you, Mrs. Galvez. Good-bye.

Mrs. Galvez: You're welcome, Peter. Good-bye.

3. Ms. Pappas: Hello.

Hector Almeda: Hello, Ms. Pappas? This is Hector Almeda. I live in Apartment 4D.

Ms. Pappas: Hello, Hector. Is everything all right?

Hector Almeda: Not really, I'm sure there's a gas leak in my apartment. I can smell gas all through my place. I think it's my gas heater. The smell is really strong around it.

| Ms. Pappas: | I'll call the gas company right away. They'll send someone out at once. While you're waiting, open your windows; then get everyone out of the apartment. |
| Hector Almeda: | OK, I'll do what you said. Thanks, Ms. Pappas. |

4.
Abby:	Oh, Mr. Aquino! Excuse me, Mr. Aquino!
Mr. Aquino:	Well, hi, Abby. What's up?
Abby:	Mr. Aquino, the lock on my back window won't work.
Mr. Aquino:	What's wrong with it?
Abby:	I can't get it to close. I think a part has fallen off. Could you fix it, please?
Mr. Aquino:	How about if I get to it tomorrow afternoon?
Abby:	Mr. Aquino, having a window that won't lock makes me uncomfortable. It makes it easy for someone to break into my apartment when I'm at work or asleep. Could you please fix it today?
Mr. Aquino:	OK, Abby. I'll take care of it this afternoon.
Abby:	Thanks, Mr. Aquino.

Listen again. Who will fix the problem? Match. *[Play the tape or read the transcript of Exercise A aloud again.]*

Exercise B.
Anna Ching is giving advice on a radio show. Look and listen. Circle *yes* or *no*.

A: Hello and welcome to Your Legal Rights. I'm your host, Ray Perez. Do you rent an apartment? Then you'll be interested in today's topic, tenants' rights. Our guest is Anna Ching. She's a consumer advocate in Roseville who specializes in tenant-landlord relationships. Welcome, Anna.

B: Thanks, Ray. I'm glad to be here.

A: So, Anna, what exactly do you do?

B: Well, Ray, my job is to help tenants, people who rent a place to live.

A: Why do tenants need help, Anna? What kind of problems do they have?

B: Well, for example, maybe there are no lights in the hallways in their building. The tenants have a hard time getting to their apartments at night. And they can't see if strangers are hiding there.

A: That's a problem.

B: And the fact is, landlords in Roseville are required by law to put lights in the public hallways of their buildings.

A: Really? Are there other things landlords are required to do?

B: Oh, yes. They must install window and door locks that are strong. And not just any kind of door lock. The locks have to be the kind that open on the outside with a key, but that you can open on the inside without a key.

A: Sure, I can see why. A person has to be able to get out without a key in case there's a fire or other danger. Are landlords responsible for anything else in addition to window and door locks?

B: Well, they must provide each apartment with some kind of emergency exit — a way to get out other than the front door.

A: You mean, like a back door or a fire escape?

B: Yes. Some sort of fire escape is really important.

A: Speaking of fire, what about smoke detectors? Are they required?

B: Absolutely. Installing smoke detectors in the building's hallways and apartments is a landlord's responsibility.

A: Are there any other safety rights that tenants have?

B: Oh, yes. Landlords must keep their buildings in good shape. They're responsible for the electrical wiring, the plumbing, and the heating systems. If anything goes wrong, they have to make sure it's fixed by a qualified person—like an electrician, a plumber, or a gas company repairman. That's the law in Roseville.

A: Well, that's about all the time we have. Do you want to add anything, Anna?

B: Yes, just remember that renting a safe home is the right of every tenant. If anyone listening wants to find out more, call the office of Tenant Affairs in City Hall. If you live outside this area, call your local tenant affairs office to find out what laws apply in your city or town.

A: Thanks, Anna. You've been listening to Anna Ching talk about tenants' rights. This is Ray Perez reminding you that when you know your legal rights, you know how to protect yourself.

Listen again. What does Anna Ching say landlords and landladies in Roseville must do? Circle the correct answers.

[Play the tape or read the transcript of Exercise B aloud again.]

Unit 8

Listening (Page 104)
Exercise A.
Look and listen. What do Dr. Patel and Evelyn Field talk about? Circle the numbers.

Dr. Patel: Good to see you, Mrs. Field. Let's see. You haven't had a check-up in a while.

Evelyn Field: Yes, I know, Dr. Patel. It's been three years since my last check-up.

Dr. Patel: Three years is a long time. How are you feeling?

Evelyn Field: Well, kind of nervous. I'm not sleeping well.

Dr. Patel: How many hours of sleep do you get each night?

Evelyn Field: About five.

Dr. Patel: Five hours, I see. And how's work? Are you under a lot of stress?

Evelyn Field: Oh, yes, come to think of it, I am. I became a supervisor six months ago, and it's a lot of work.

Dr. Patel: You know, Mrs. Field, one way to control stress, and to help yourself sleep better, is to exercise. How much exercise do you get?

Evelyn Field: I walk to work. It takes about ten minutes.

Dr. Patel: That's good, but you need more exercise than just walking to work. I know you have a busy schedule, but you ought to get more exercise. Another question, Mrs. Field. How's your diet? Are you eating well-balanced meals?

Evelyn Field: Well, maybe. During the day I usually eat donuts and sandwiches from the vending machines. At night I grab a hamburger.

Dr. Patel: Donuts, sandwiches, and hamburgers. That's it?

Evelyn Field: Yes. And I drink a lot of coffee.

Dr. Patel: The coffee is probably making you nervous. You'd better think about making some changes in your eating habits. Let's finish the check-up. Then we can talk about how you can take better care of yourself.

Listen again. What does Mrs. Field tell Dr. Patel about her health habits? Circle the answer. *[Play the tape or read the transcript of Exercise A aloud again.]*

Exercise B.
Benny Sakata is a famous rock star. Right now he's being interviewed on *Spotlight!* Look and listen. Circle *yes* or *no.*

A: Hello, fans! Welcome to Spotlight! I'm Alma Vega, bringing the stars out of the skies and into your home! Tonight I'm talking to Benny Sakata, lead singer for the rock band Crazylegs. Benny, so good to see you again!

B: Glad to be here, Alma.

A: What are you up to these days, Benny?

B: Currently I'm on a concert tour.

A: That must mean a lot of traveling and sleepless nights.

B: Lots of traveling, yes. We're going all around the country. But I do manage to get enough sleep.

A: Enough sleep? On a concert tour?

B: Sure. I sleep from four in the morning until noon.

A: How about exercise, Benny, and well-balanced meals? Do you get enough of those?

B: Yes. I think eating well and getting enough exercise give me the energy I need for my concerts.

A: What kind of exercise do you like?

B: I jog 2 to 3 miles every day.

A: Do you do anything else to keep healthy?

B: Well, I recently gave up coffee.

A: What about check-ups? Do you get regular check-ups?

B: No, I don't. I know I should, but it's really hard with a schedule like mine.

A: Well, Benny, thanks for telling us what's going on with you. We hope you'll check in again with *Spotlight!*

Unit 9

Listening (Page 118)
Exercise A.
An employer will often talk to workers about how well they are doing on the job. This is called a performance review. Three employees are having their performance reviews. Look and listen. Write their jobs in column A.

1. A: Ms. Mendoza?

   B: Yes, come in. Oh, hello, Mary. You're here for your performance review, aren't you?

   A: Yes, I am. Am I too early?

   B: No, this is fine. Come in. Have a seat. It's always a pleasure to do your performance reviews. You're one of our best cashiers.

   A: Thank you, Ms. Mendoza. I'm happy to hear that.

   B: You have a very good attitude, Mary. That's one thing that makes you such a valuable employee.

   A: It's easy to have a good attitude here. I like my job as a cashier. I enjoy working with people.

   B: Good. We've also noticed that you're very responsible.

   A: Thank you.

   B: Now, let's discuss your salary. We're offering you a raise of $100 per month.

   A: A raise? I wasn't expecting that. Thank you very much.

B: You've earned it, Mary.

2. A: Good morning, Lester. Do you have some time this morning for your performance review?

   B: Good morning, Lily. Yes, I do. I planned for it.

   A: Come on in my office. Please have a seat, Lester.

   B: Thank you.

   A: You know, Lester, you're a good secretary. You're a very careful worker, and that's important in your job.

   B: Thank you, Lily. It's nice of you to say that. I enjoy this kind of work, too.

   A: That's great. There is one thing you need to improve, though. I've noticed that you're often late. Are you having some trouble getting here in the mornings?

   B: Well, my wife hasn't been able to drop the kids off at school the last few weeks, so I've had to do it. But she'll be taking them again starting next week.

   A: All right, Lester. I thought there might be some problem. I'm glad you're solving it. I really need you here on time. You know how much I depend on you.

   B: I know.

   A: One other thing. You're probably wondering about a promotion. I'm not offering you one now because I think you still have things to learn. But we'll discuss a promotion at your next review.

   B: That makes sense. Thank you, Lily.

3. A: Lou, can you come in here for a moment?

   B: Sure, Gil. I just finished my shift.

   A: Great. Have a seat, Lou. I was thinking . . . you've been a waiter here for over a year now, right?

   B: Yes, it's been a year and two months.

   A: Well, you're an excellent employee. You're very reliable, and you get along well with the customers. As a matter of fact, you're one of the best waiters I've ever had work for me.

   B: Well, thanks for saying that, Gil.

   A: You're welcome. Anyway, you know that Ken is leaving next month to go back to school. I need a headwaiter to take his place. I think you're the one for the job. Are you interested in the promotion?

B: Yes, I am.

A: That's great. I'd like you to take a class in restaurant management. The restaurant will pay for the course. Are you willing to go to the classes?

B: Of course. I want to get more education, and I'm very interested in restaurant management.

A: OK. I think there's a class starting soon at the junior college. I'd like you to get into that class. I can make the promotion official next month, when Ken leaves.

B: Will the class be over by then?

A: No, but that's OK. I know I can count on you to finish the class.

B: Yes, you can, Gil. Thank you very much for this opportunity.

A: You're welcome, Lou. You've earned it.

Listen again. What do their employers say about them? Circle the answers in column B. *[Play the tape or read the transcript of Exercise A aloud again.]*

Listen again. What happens? Circle the answers in column C. *[Play the tape or read the transcript of Exercise A aloud again.]*

Exercise B.
Katya and Ed are talking about their career goals. Look and listen. Complete the chart.

Katya: Hi, Ed.

Ed: Hi, Katya. Where are you going?

Katya: I'm on my way to my word-processing class.

Ed: Word-processing class? I thought you worked as a receptionist.

Katya: I do. I'm a receptionist for the Downing Company. I'm taking word-processing classes so I can get a promotion. I want to be a secretary.

Ed: I see. That sounds great. Will you make more money?

Katya: Yes, I will. How's your job going? Are you still working at Food World?

Ed: Yes, I am. I was promoted to cashier six months ago. I'd like to be an accountant some day, but it'll take a while, I think.

Katya: You know, my school has accounting classes. Maybe if you take them, the store will promote you.

Ed: Accounting classes? That's a great idea.

Katya: The store might even pay for them. Lots of companies pay for employee education. They're happy that you want to learn more about the business.

Ed: Is your company paying for your word-processing classes?

Katya: The company pays half and I pay the other half.

Ed: That's pretty good. I think I'll ask my boss if Food World will pay for accounting classes.

Katya: Even if the store won't pay for it, you can probably still take the classes. The junior college isn't very expensive.

Ed: I'll look into it. Thanks, Katya. And good luck in your word-processing class.

Katya: Thanks, Ed. Bye!

Listen again. What kind of training will they need? Circle. *[Play the tape or read the transcript of Exercise B aloud again.]*

Unit 10

Listening (Page 132)
Exercise A.
Look and listen. What's the problem with their cars? Circle the answer.

1. A: Auto Repair Service. This is Linda Torres. How may I help you?

   B: Hi, Linda. This is Doris Morita. I've had a problem with my oil light for about a month. It keeps coming on.

   A: Maybe your car needs oil. Have you checked it lately?

   B: Oh, yes. And I add oil whenever the light comes on. But it keeps coming on.

   A: Your car is probably burning oil too fast.

   B: What should I do?

   A: Bring your car in and I'll check the engine. Your car might also need a tune-up.

   B: OK. I'll bring it in. When would be a good time?

   A: How about tomorrow morning at eight?

B:　That'd be fine. See you then. Thanks, Linda.

2. A:　Tell me again what the problem is, Ben.

B:　Sometimes I have trouble starting the car. Other times, it starts without trouble.

A:　I bet it's your battery.

B:　But, Al, this battery's only a year old. And it's guaranteed for three years.

A:　Well, some batteries don't last as long as their warranty. Anyway, why take chances? You ought to get a new battery. I can give you one for a good price.

B:　Al, I can tell from my headlights that the battery is fine.

A:　Well, you never know. If I were you, I'd have my battery checked as soon as possible. Let's see, I can fit you in tomorrow afternoon.

B:　Hold on, Al. Let me think about this, please.

A:　OK, but don't wait too long.

B:　I'll let you know what I decide.

3. A:　Hi, Carl's Repair Shop. What can I do for you today?

B:　Hello, Carl. This is Mrs. Solera. I think something's wrong with my car. I've heard screeching noises for several days whenever I stop. It sounds like metal scraping metal. And now I smell something burning—like rubber.

A:　Screeching noises and a smell of burning rubber?

B:　Yes.

A:　Well, it sounds as if it's your brakes. You might just need to put in some brake fluid.

B:　I see. I'll check the brake fluid then.

A:　That'd be a good idea. If you need some, go ahead and add it. But, bring your car in anyway, and I'll check the brakes for you.

B:　Thanks, Carl.

Listen again. What advice does each mechanic give? *[Play the tape or read the transcript of Exercise A aloud again.]*

Exercise B.
Rita just bought a car. What does the salesman say she should do to take care of her car? Circle the answers.

Rita:　Congratulations Rita. I know you'll really enjoy your new car. Make sure you take good care of it.

Don:　Thanks Don. I want to make sure it'll last a long time. Do you have any advice?

Rita:　Yes. The most important thing is to change the oil regularly.

Don:　How often should I change the oil?

Rita:　About once every three months.

Don:　Is there anything else I should do?

Rita:　Yes. You should get a complete tune-up once a year, and you should check the radiator regularly to make sure it has enough water.

Rita:　Thanks for all your help, Don.

Don:　Good luck, Rita.